"What are

Clutching the sheet, Kelly pulled herself up against the satin pillows, a stricken look on her face.

"I believe it's my hotel room," Max said on a sigh. "As to why I'm in bed with you, I'm not sure. Frankly, this is as big a shock to me as it is to you. You know, I don't make a habit of waking up next to strange women."

"I hope you don't think *I've* done this sort of thing before!"

"Of course not," Max agreed hastily. "It was all a game we were playing, right?"

She had intended to take him up on his dare, flirt a bit and then walk away. Instead, his tempting smile had gotten to her. Like Cinderella, she should've run away from him at midnight. Just when had the game turned into something more serious? And, more to the point, what had she gotten herself into?

Dear Reader,

February is a month made for romance, and here at Harlequin American Romance we invite *you* to be our Valentine!

Every month, we bring you four reasons to celebrate romance, and beloved author Muriel Jensen has reasons of her own—*Four Reasons for Fatherhood*, to be precise. Join former workaholic Aaron Bradley as he learns about parenthood—and love—from four feisty youngsters and one determined lady in the finale to our exciting miniseries THE DADDY CLUB.

Some men just have a way with women, and our next two heroes are no exception. In Pamela Bauer's *Corporate Cowboy*, when Austin Bennett hits his head and loses his memory, Kacy Judd better watch out—because her formerly arrogant boss is suddenly the most irresistible man in town! And in *Married by Midnight* by Mollie Molay, Maxwell Taylor has more charm than even he suspects—he goes to a wedding one day, and wakes up married the next!

And if you're wondering HOW TO MARRY... *The World's Best Dad*, look no farther than Valerie Taylor's heartwarming tale. Julie Miles may not follow her own advice, but she's got gorgeous Ben Harbison's attention anyway!

We hope you enjoy every romantic minute of our four wonderful stories.

Warm wishes,

Melissa Jeglinski
Associate Senior Editor

Married by Midnight

MOLLIE MOLAY

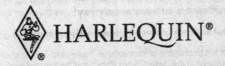

HARLEQUIN®

TORONTO • NEW YORK • LONDON
AMSTERDAM • PARIS • SYDNEY • HAMBURG
STOCKHOLM • ATHENS • TOKYO • MILAN • MADRID
PRAGUE • WARSAW • BUDAPEST • AUCKLAND

For Paul and Terri Molé, whose wedding inspired this story. And to newly married Michael and Lynn Fox. Great grandsons who were smart enough to marry wonderful women.
Way to go!

ISBN 0-373-16815-2

MARRIED BY MIDNIGHT

Copyright © 2000 by Mollie Molé.

Visit us at www.romance.net

Printed in U.S.A.

ABOUT THE AUTHOR

After working for a number of years as a Logistics Contract Administrator in the aircraft industry, Mollie Molay turned to a career she found far more satisfying—writing romance novels. Mollie lives in Northridge, California, surrounded by her two daughters and seven grandchildren, many of whom find their way into her books. She enjoys hearing from her readers and welcomes comments. You can write to her c/o Harlequin Books, 300 East 42nd Street, 6th floor, New York, NY 10017.

Books by Mollie Molay

HARLEQUIN AMERICAN ROMANCE

560—FROM DRIFTER TO DADDY
597—HER TWO HUSBANDS
616—MARRIAGE BY MISTAKE
638—LIKE FATHER, LIKE SON
682—NANNY & THE BODYGUARD
703—OVERNIGHT WIFE
729—WANTED: DADDY
776—FATHER IN TRAINING
799—DADDY BY CHRISTMAS
815—MARRIED BY MIDNIGHT

Don't miss any of our special offers. Write to us at the following address for information on our newest releases.

Harlequin Reader Service
U.S.: 3010 Walden Ave., P.O. Box 1325, Buffalo, NY 14269
Canadian: P.O. Box 609, Fort Erie, Ont. L2A 5X3

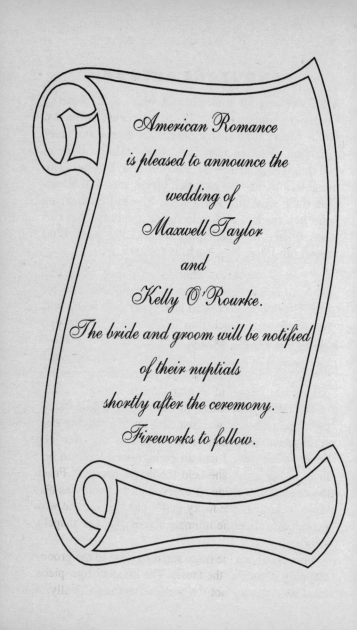

American Romance
is pleased to announce the
wedding of
Maxwell Taylor
and
Kelly O'Rourke.
The bride and groom will be notified
of their nuptials
shortly after the ceremony.
Fireworks to follow.

Prologue

Max Taylor didn't know what hit him.

Caught in a logjam of cheering wedding guests, he was nursing a glass of champagne punch when suddenly an object flew through the air. He ducked—too late. The bride's decorated lace garter, still warm with her body heat, struck him just above his right eye. Shaken out of his reverie, Max instinctively reached for the garter and caught it before it fell into the punch bowl. The crowd around him parted and to his bewilderment started to clap and cheer him on.

To complicate matters, directly in his line of vision, the maid of honor was seated with her striking emerald-green bridesmaid's dress drawn up over her knees, a leg poised and an embarrassed look on her face. In her arms, she held the bridal bouquet. From the eager expressions on everyone's faces, it was obvious to him, as the lucky garter-catcher, that he was expected to slide the intimate object over her shapely slender leg.

Max could see the bride standing next to the groom clapping in time to the music. The amateur four-piece band was playing not too well but enthusiastically.

With the drummer executing a brisk roll of the drums, the master of ceremonies motioned Max forward and pointed to the redhead's upper thigh.

Max froze.

What was he to do now?

A whirlwind of thoughts raced through his mind, including making a quick getaway. He should have been pleased. After all, this was the first time he'd won anything more than a few bucks on a lottery ticket. Good enough, he muttered to himself as he gazed at the sculptured leg, but why did the prize have to be something that might test his manhood? He hesitated, trying to come up with a good reason to decline the honor. He couldn't. The groom was his cousin and he was the best man. Family honor was at stake. Short of causing a scene, he realized he had to be a good sport and enter into the festivities.

He took a deep breath, raised his glass to his lips and gulped the last of the champagne punch for courage. Fortified, he handed the glass to his nearest neighbor and moved inside the circle of clapping wedding guests. Up close, the leg's owner looked watchful. He didn't blame her. Although they were part of the wedding party, they'd only seen each other for the first time at the brief rehearsal last night. What he was about to do *was* pretty intimate.

He knelt on the one good knee he had left after his recent skiing accident, carefully removed the lady's dainty shoe and slowly slid the garter over her stockinged foot, up her silken leg and to her knee. He felt himself flush when he became more aware of her charms than he cared to admit. He stopped and started to get to his feet.

''No, no, no,'' the wedding guests chanted.

''Up, up, up, up,'' the master of ceremonies instructed, sending Max back down on his knee and firmly pointing the way.

Max took another deep breath, glanced apologetically at his fellow victim and slid the garter upward another inch.

''More, more, more,'' urged the crowd.

Max silently muttered his frustration and cautiously moved the garter up another inch, and another. His body warmed with each move. The innuendos thrown at him weren't helping his discomfiture a damn bit. By the time he'd reached her warm upper thigh, he'd had more than any red-blooded man could be expected to handle and he wasn't going to take it anymore. He enjoyed a joke as well as any other man, but since he didn't know the lady he was touching so intimately, this was too much. He muttered his apology and hoped for the best.

Chapter One

The pressure of a creamy, petal-soft feminine shoulder cuddled against his chest shocked Max out of his dream. A dream where a copper-haired enchantress was brushing a hand across his bare shoulder, and hazel-green eyes shone with invitation. Disoriented, Max allowed his gaze to travel down a slender arm to a sculptured waist and an enticingly curved hip that was partially covered by the white satin bedsheet.

Max froze. The last thing he remembered clearly was the ridiculous garter ceremony at his cousin's wedding. But never in his wildest imagination had he anticipated a moment like this.

The unexpected but pleasant discovery explained why he'd awakened satiated, at peace with the world. He leaned over and took a closer look. The intriguing view caused his body to respond in ways he was embarrassed to contemplate.

One thing for sure, Kelly O'Rourke, the twenty-two-year-old maid of honor at last night's wedding and owner of the most beautiful pair of legs he'd ever seen, was the last woman Max expected to find in his bed.

He leaned back against the pillows and tried to remember how and why he and Kelly were in bed together.

The winter wedding between his cousin, Troy Taylor, and DeeDee Connor, and the tumultuous celebration that had followed last night had been one for the books. He could barely recall what had happened after he'd caught the bride's garter and slid it up the maid of honor's leg. After that, events had passed in a blur.

Maybe it had been because he'd caught the last flight from Boston to Las Vegas. Upon arriving, instead of catching up on his sleep, he'd gotten caught up in a hasty wedding rehearsal, Troy's bachelor party and the ensuing wedding festivities. Going without sleep for thirty-six hours and operating on sheer momentum, as he was, little wonder he'd been done in by the potent champagne punch.

He eyed Kelly cautiously. She was bound to be frosted when she awakened.

The last thing he *did* remember clearly was catching the bridal garter. He remembered sliding the lace confection over Kelly's warm and slender leg while the other wedding guests egged him on. His frank admiration for the silk-clad leg he held had seemed harmless enough to him, but not to Kelly. To his surprise, the warning look in her eyes had held a message. Somewhere along the line, a dare had been cast and, heaven help him, accepted.

One step at a time, he told himself as he struggled to remember what had happened next. One step at a time. The rest of the story was bound to come to him if he relaxed and let the answers flow when they were ready.

He took a deep breath and surveyed his surroundings. He was pretty sure he was in the Las Vegas Majestic Hotel where the Taylor-Connor wedding and reception had taken place. But he was surprised he'd booked anything as lush as these surroundings. Obviously he had; his suitcase sat beside the bed.

With its mirrored ceiling and white satin linens the bedroom was part of a luxurious two-room suite. A trail of masculine and feminine shoes led to the bed. His clothing was thrown haphazardly over a chair and an emerald-green bridesmaid's dress, along with a lacy bra and matching bikini, was flung across the foot of the bed. Silken hose were draped over a bed lamp like a victory flag.

Through the open folding doors, he saw a sitting room with all the accoutrements of a posh lodging. A giant-screen TV, a man-size upholstered couch and matching love seat filled the center of the room. A bridal bouquet lay wilting on the coffee table, alongside a short wisp of a bridal veil. He remembered Kelly catching the bouquet, all right, but what was DeeDee's bridal veil doing here?

Puzzled, he looked at the couch in the center of the next room. He seemed to remember he'd gone to sleep there sometime last night. Why had he chosen the couch when he had a king-size bed waiting for him? He glanced down at his sleeping companion. The bigger question was when and how he had wound up in bed with her.

He fought a growing uneasiness as he tried hard to recall what *had* actually happened last night. Slowly, the mental clouds began to clear. He recalled Kelly's warning look as he'd slid the garter up her leg. He also recalled her look that dared him to a point where he'd been driven by an uncommon impulse to change the warning to a look of desire.

He gazed at the rumpled bed and the clothing strewn haphazardly around the room. From the looks of things, he'd obviously accomplished his goal only too well. Too bad he didn't remember the details.

But couch or no couch, good intentions or otherwise, it didn't take much imagination to figure out he and Kelly had ultimately fallen into bed together. The evidence was obvious enough to make him wonder how he could possibly have drawn a blank after what surely must have been a memorable night.

He gazed down at Kelly's ivory and pink-tinged skin. Wrapped in a white satin sheet, her shoulders bare, she looked every bit as enticing as she had during the garter incident. And, heaven help him, in his dream.

Her lips, curved in a smile, were moving soundlessly. He leaned over to listen. The smile and the possible meaning behind it sent a wave of guilt through him.

After all, from what little he remembered, he'd only intended to tease, to challenge Kelly. One look had led to another, closer one until the game they'd been playing had become more than a simple flirtation. Now the burning question was what had happened during the night to leave her with a smile on her face.

She looked so sweet, so natural, it was hard to imagine this was the same feisty woman who had taken on his wordless challenge last night. Impulsively, he gently brushed an auburn eyelash from her cheek.

Never one to run away from a problem he'd helped to create, Max cleared his throat.

Kelly stirred at the sound. It was a few moments before she opened her eyes. "You!"

"I'm afraid so," Max agreed, inching sideways at the edge in her voice. If there was going to be a disagreement, he intended to stay out of arm's reach.

Clutching the sheet, Kelly pulled herself up against the satin pillows. "What are you doing here?"

Max heaved a sigh of relief. She was taking things more calmly than he'd expected. "If you're talking about the room, I believe it's mine. As to why I'm here in bed with you, I'm not sure. I just woke up myself." When she looked confused, he added, "By the way, under the circumstances, you can call me Max."

"I'm Kelly," she replied, biting her lip. Her mind whirled with questions, questions she was too embarrassed to ask. One thing was clear, she was in bed with Troy's best man. A twenty-six-year-old businessman DeeDee had urged on her before the wedding ceremony. At first, she hadn't been interested—but things had obviously changed.

Kelly gazed at his rumpled brown hair, the dark shadows on his cheeks and his broad, tanned shoulders. In spite of her embarrassment, her gaze slowly moved down his bare shoulders, to the golden brown curls on his chest and down to his lithe waist. Warm memories flooded her mind.

She remembered taking him up on his unspoken

sensual challenge, intending to put him in his place. Instead, she'd wound up falling for his sexy smile.

In spite of her dismay at finding herself in bed with Max, the warm glow lingering in her middle brought back memories of his sensuous glances and dynamite kisses.

Those same glances were warming her now.

Max's eyes suddenly widened. She was just in time to grab the satin sheet and keep it from sliding to her waist. "I'm not sure how things got started last night," she muttered as she pulled the sheet to her chin, "but it seems you won. I never planned on going this far. I sure didn't start out intending to spend the night with you."

Max rubbed his forehead. "Frankly, this is as big a surprise to me as it is to you." He gazed at the silk stockings hanging on the lamp and grinned sheepishly. "I honestly don't seem to remember much about last night, either. Maybe it was because I was pretty exhausted after we—"

"Stop! Stop right there!" Kelly warned as memories of a killer smile, tangled limbs and heated kisses filled her mind. "I don't think I care to hear the details. It must have been the champagne punch," she muttered. "I've never done anything like this before."

"Me neither. My behavior last night was totally unlike me, too." He'd had his share of relationships, but until now he'd always been awake to enjoy them. What had possessed him to play erotic games with the bride's best friend? Mentally cursing himself for his stupidity, he forced a feeble smile. "In spite of how this looks, the last thing I remember was offering to sleep on the couch last night.''

Kelly glanced from the undisturbed couch to the tousled bed, to the clothing strewn around the room. She frowned. "I can't believe I did this."

"It was all just a game we were playing, right?" Max said hastily.

Kelly decided to play it safe. "Maybe."

"Maybe? Does that mean you remember what happened last night?"

"Just enough," she answered, turning a deeper shade of pink at how much she actually did remember.

She *had* intended to take him up on his dare, flirt a bit and then walk away. Instead, before she'd realized what was happening, his tempting smile had gotten to her. Like Cinderella, she should have walked away from him at midnight.

Just when had the game turned into something more serious? And more to the point, what had she gotten herself into?

Eyeing Kelly's flushed face and her obvious dismay, Max swallowed the light remark he had been about to make. As he mentally reviewed the last twelve hours, a lightbulb turned on in his head. Maybe the one important detail he *did* remember would mitigate some of the more obvious evidence of what had taken place last night.

He took a deep breath. "I think we may have gotten married last night."

"Married! That's ridiculous. Why would I have married you? I don't even know you!" She pulled the sheet closer around her and inched to the edge of the bed.

"Maybe so," Max agreed. "But during the hotel's unexpected celebration of Troy and DeeDee's marriage, I think something happened. Something that involved us."

"That's enough," Kelly said hurriedly, putting up a hand to stop him. "Try to remember. It was all a game. I'd rather forget last night, and all of this, too." She glanced down at the bed.

"Maybe so," Max went on doggedly. "But I swear I remember a wedding ceremony."

"Not ours," Kelly replied firmly. "I couldn't have gotten that carried away, not even by you. I'm not ready to be married."

Max decided maybe it wasn't the right time or place to tell Kelly he'd dreamed of making love to the woman he thought was his wife. But the dream had felt so real. "Maybe you're right, but I can't shake the memory of our marriage ceremony."

"Impossible! If we'd gotten married, I'd remember. I told you, I'm not ready to be married and I meant it."

"Okay, have it your way," he said. "But I want to go on record." He raised his right hand. "I swear that the one thing I do remember clearly is offering to sleep on the couch. You do remember that much, don't you?"

The look in his deep brown eyes was sincere, but something told her he hadn't remained on the couch for long. Or, considering the way her body was still tingling, maybe he hadn't gone to sleep there at all.

Under the covers, Kelly was investigating her

thigh. The bridal garter that seemed to have started the whole mess was still in place. But to her dismay, the garter was all she had on!

She groaned as she envisioned her father, her three brothers and assorted members of her family accusing her of conduct unbecoming an O'Rourke. Not that they would be entirely wrong. Awakening to find herself in a strange hotel room, completely unclothed and in bed with a man she'd only met last night was definitely an O'Rourke no-no.

"Are you sure you remember the details about…um…last night?" She felt herself flush as she spoke.

"Not enough," Max muttered, "but I'm sure there's an explanation somewhere." He slowly edged away from Kelly before she could realize he didn't have any clothing on under the covers either. Not even his socks.

The growing look of dismay Kelly was giving him spelled big trouble. He wished he could offer some kind of explanation that would give them both a graceful way out of the obvious, but he couldn't. The indisputable fact remained, they'd wound up in bed together. And the only answer he could come up with was one she didn't want to hear: Kelly was his wife, and they'd consummated their wedding night.

"Max, what are we going to do about this? We have to talk."

"I couldn't agree more." He wasn't looking forward to trying to explain the unexplainable, but trying to would at least be a step in the right direction. He could apologize, but that was closing the proverbial barn door after the horse was gone. Besides, Kelly didn't look in the mood to try to understand, forgive and forget the impulse that may have sent them before a preacher.

He told himself Kelly would eventually cool down and listen to reason. If they'd actually gotten married, he was ready to suggest civilized goodbyes and an annulment. Or, he swallowed hard at the thought, a divorce.

"Maybe no one knows about this but us," he offered with a feeble smile. "I'm willing to forget last night if you are. How about you?"

Kelly thought hard. What had apparently been a romantic thing to do last night, in broad daylight became an irresponsible scenario. In all fairness, she couldn't put all the blame on Max. He may have started the flirtation, but he was obviously a lot more worldly than she was. She'd been a fool to think she could outsmart him. Besides, it took two people to get into a situation like this.

The problem was that DeeDee had talked so much about Max and how much they had in common, Kelly had turned her off. Now that she realized Max was the sexiest man she'd ever met up with, maybe she should have listened to her friend.

She already had a controlling father and two older brothers who insisted on looking after her. The last thing she needed was another man in her life. Even one like Max.

Another unhappy thought hit her. The O'Rourkes were a large extended and prolific Irish family. She had an army of cousins, most of them male, and had been around them often enough to have heard enough stories that had made her blush. What if she'd gotten pregnant after last night?

"Something wrong?"

"Maybe," Kelly whispered. She bit her lip as one unhappy thought led to another. How do you ask a man if he'd used protection last night? "Did you, er..." She took a deep breath and plunged into deep waters. "Did you use protection last night?"

Max swallowed hard. If he'd actually thought Kelly was his wife, maybe not. On the other hand, maybe yes. He *had* had a condom in his wallet. "Yes. I don't think I could have been that irresponsible," he replied frankly. He made a mental note to check his wallet as soon as he was alone.

Before they could pursue the subject, there was a knock on the door.

"Who's that?" Kelly whispered, looking around for cover. "I can't let anyone find me here."

"Maybe if we don't answer, they'll think we're still asleep and go away," Max said under his breath. He put a finger to his lips.

The knock sounded again, this time louder.

"No such luck," Max muttered. "I guess we'll never know who it is unless I answer the door." He had a bare leg out from under the covers when he realized he couldn't reach his clothes. The fact that they were in a tangled mess on the floor surprised him. He was normally an organized man, a man who never gave in to impulse. Something had happened last night to change him.

"Maybe you'd better close your eyes for a minute."

"I will not!"

He raised his eyebrows in a sardonic question and pointed to the jumble of clothing. "My clothes are down there."

Kelly moaned and slid under the blankets.

Max dashed for his trousers, put them on and made for the door before some lunatic broke it down. "Who's there?"

"Reggie Bennett, the assistant manager of the hotel, sir. You and Mrs. Taylor checked in too late last night to receive the usual amenities that come with the bridal suite. I have them for you now."

Max felt himself blanch as he shrugged into his shirt and shoes. *Mrs. Taylor? Bridal suite?* So, last night hadn't entirely been a dream. Like it or not, he *had* married Kelly.

Max groaned. He was a man who enjoyed the company of women, but marriage had been the farthest thing from his mind. And the last thing on his carefully plotted life's agenda.

He took a deep breath. Even with those disturbing memories of a marriage ceremony, he wasn't exactly ready to believe this marriage business. If he'd gotten married, surely he would have had to have had a marriage license and a marriage certificate, wouldn't he?

After making sure Kelly couldn't be seen from the door, he held it open a crack. The assistant manager met his gaze with a broad smile. "Our apologies, sir. The management of the Majestic Hotel would like to correct our unfortunate oversight."

Oversight? Max's heart plummeted when he realized daylight was shining through the shuttered windows. Somehow, he'd misplaced a large chunk of the day. And, in the interim, he must have somehow acquired a bride and, heaven help him, consummated the marriage.

"May we come in now?"

Max took another look behind him before he opened the outer door. A room-service waiter rolled in a linen-covered cart and positioned two chairs next to it.

Entranced, Max studied the gaily decorated cart. As Bennett had announced, there was a wedding breakfast in all its glory, including a bottle of champagne in an iced silver container and pats of butter in the form of hearts. A cut-glass vase held a dozen white roses. To his increasing dismay, a congratulatory message was prominently propped against the vase.

What further blew his mind were the silver and gold balloons in the shape of wedding bells that floated behind the cart.

"Our apologies for the delay in bringing your breakfast, Mr. Taylor. After what happened last night, we weren't sure you and Mrs. Taylor were up yet." A humorous glint came into Reggie Bennett's eyes as he regarded Max's open shirt. "If there's anything else you would like, please don't hesitate to ask." He left with a broad smile.

After what happened last night? A dim recollection of shouting people and flashing cameras floated through Max's mind. What worse could possibly have happened?

"Max, are they gone?" Kelly called impatiently.

"Yes, but not before they left us breakfast," he replied. His stomach churned as he eyed the bottle of champagne on ice. Champagne had been his downfall last night. He heard Kelly mutter under her breath.

She had to be upset if she'd heard Bennett. For a woman who firmly refused to believe she was married, what would she do when she actually saw the cart?

"I'm not that hungry," Kelly said. "I'll get dressed and we can decide what to do."

As far as Max was concerned, discussions had to wait. What he had to do first was find out how and when he'd actually acquired a wife. He eyed the outside door for a quick getaway. "I'll be back in a minute," he announced and rushed out the door.

When Kelly heard the door close, she peered into the next room. The sight of the floating bell-shaped balloons brought her marching into the room.

Then she saw the bridal veil on the coffee table. If this was intended to be a joke, and if Max was in on it, it wasn't funny.

Married? No way! Max might believe they were married, but she knew better. Right now she needed a long, hot bath and time to plan some course of action to end this nonsense.

Music began to play when she opened the door to the bathroom. She was rendered speechless by a giant Jacuzzi strategically placed in front of a mirrored wall. Tropical plants hung from a skylight above the tub. A shelf held jars of bath oils and colorful soaps in the shapes of flowers. There were assorted brushes to wash one's back and, to Kelly's growing discomfiture, bottles of assorted perfumes and ointments clearly intended for rituals of love. Her middle warmed at the sensual implications of a jar marked Aromatic Body Butter.

Visions of Max rubbing her body with the scented

butter, and her mental reactions to the idea of his
unclothed body, were more than she could bring herself to safely contemplate. Thank goodness he wasn't
here to see the Arabian Nights scene in front of her.

To her relief, on a more practical level, fluffy white
bathrobes, embroidered with ''Mr.'' and ''Mrs.,''
waited on a padded bench.

She turned on the water and sat down on the edge
of the Jacuzzi. One by one, she picked up the tiny
colored balls of bath oil beside the faucet and dropped
them into the water. The scent that began to waft
through the room turned her thoughts to sensual
games. Games she would have wanted to play if she
were actually honeymooning with the man she loved.

The bathroom was obviously an elaborate setting
for a seduction scene, she thought wistfully as she
slid into the water. But the truth was that, in spite of
last night's apparent foolishness, she wasn't out to
seduce anyone. Max Taylor least of all. As soon as
he returned, she intended to tell him so.

Chapter Two

Muttering to himself, Max made his way to the hotel's executive offices on the first floor. How could he be a married man if he didn't even remember applying for a wedding license?

He shook his head. He wasn't ready to believe he *was* a married man anyway. And as for Kelly, she didn't seem all that jazzed up about the idea of being his wife, either.

As for spending last night in bed together—he rechecked his wallet to reassure himself the condom was gone. Marriage to a stranger was bad enough, but a baby?

With emotionally distant parents like his own, his childhood had been nothing to rave about. As a result, he wasn't sold on fatherhood. He didn't want to start a family until he was good and ready. He wasn't ready yet.

He skidded to a stop in the center of the ornate hotel lobby. The pale blue walls were covered with reproductions of well-known landscapes. Live trees and flowering shrubs grew in the center of a courtyard fronting the check-in desk. A waterfall fell gracefully into a small stream and disappeared beneath rocks. Sunlight streamed in from skylights. The effect was that of a pastoral spring scene. Soft, romantic music played in the background. The new hotel was unlike any Las Vegas hotel he'd ever been in. No wonder he'd been carried away by the romantic ambience last night.

The scene looked vaguely familiar. Good, he thought, this might be an excellent place to fill in the gaps in his memory.

"Must have been some party," he remarked to a housekeeping-staff member tugging potted plants into place.

"You ought to know." The man chuckled. "You and your lady sure were star attractions last night."

Star attractions? Max's heart sank as he gazed around the lobby. No new flashes of memory hit him, but if there was a reasonable explanation of what had gone on last night, he intended to find it. The obvious place to start was with his cousin Troy, whose wedding seemed to have changed Max's life. He started toward a bank of public telephones, before he realized Troy and his new bride were off on an extended honeymoon, destination unknown.

Damn! Who else could he question about what he'd gotten into last night without looking like a jerk? His Aunt Clara, Troy's mother? Nah. His reputation in the Taylor family would be shot to hell. The door to that avenue closed abruptly.

He was about to go back and grill the cleaning crew, when Reggie Bennett appeared at his side. "Can I be of help, Mr. Taylor?"

"This is sure one hell of a mess, isn't it?" Max

muttered. Frustrated and unsure of what questions he could ask Bennett without sounding like a fool, he raked his fingers through his hair. In the background he heard renewed laughter.

"No problem." Bennett beamed. "We'll have everything to rights in no time. I have to tell you, the additional publicity you and Mrs. Taylor generated for the hotel last night was worth a million."

Max couldn't bring himself to tell the man he wasn't referring to the condition of the hotel lobby. Nor to ask what publicity the man was talking about. His gut feeling was that somehow he and Kelly had been involved.

He searched his memory. He could remember his initial fatal attraction to Kelly during the garter ceremony, all right. But after that his jet lag must have kicked in, because the rest of the night had passed in a haze.

The one thing he couldn't bring himself to ask Bennett about was what he and Kelly had actually done to make last night's publicity so successful. Or what would have moved the hotel's housekeeping staff to laughter. How could a man ask another man about what had happened on his own wedding night?

Gritting his teeth, Max half-heartedly thanked Bennett and turned back to the bank of elevators. In his frustration, he repeatedly poked the up button. Kelly would be waiting for him to make an accounting of his disappearance. From the sound of her voice when he'd left, he wasn't looking forward to their reunion.

A DO-NOT-DISTURB SIGN hung on the door to the bridal suite, a sure indicator Kelly meant business. He took a deep breath and opened the door to find Kelly, barefoot and wrapped in a white chenille bathrobe, pacing the floor. She was still flushed from her bath, and an exotic scent of perfume clung to her. Her lustrous red hair hung in damp tendrils around her shoulders. From the glimpse he caught of one shapely leg, she was bare under the robe. His senses began to stir before he caught a glimpse of the expression in her eyes.

"Where have you been?"

The cold look Kelly gave him would have frozen a lesser man.

"Downstairs." He closed the door behind him. The last thing he needed was an argument; his head was pounding already. "Before you start on me, let me tell you I'm not too happy about all of this either. So take it easy." He strode into the room and headed for the telephone. "The coffee's cold by now. I'm sure we'll both feel better after we have some breakfast." He picked up the phone, dialed room service and ordered a fresh pot of coffee.

"How can you think of food when we have something more important to resolve?"

He didn't know how to answer that question either, but at least having breakfast was something to do. "I think better on a full stomach. It's been a long time since I had anything decent to eat. Hors d'oeuvres and champagne punch last night doesn't cut it."

Kelly sniffed her disdain. "Go ahead and eat if you want to, but we have to talk. I intend to put this foolishness about our being married to rest right now. I'll say this again. We are not married!"

In spite of the seriousness of the situation, Max had

to smile at Kelly. The angrier she got, the more attractive she became. He started to reply, when a tattoo of sharp knocks on the door interrupted him.

"Not again," Kelly said, marching to the door. "This had better be good!" she shouted as she flung it open. "Didn't you see the sign on the door?"

A teenage boy barreled into the room. "Kelly! Quick, hide! Dad and Damon are on their way up! They're on the warpath!"

"Sean? What are you doing here?" Kelly's face was a study in surprise as she craned her neck to look over the boy's shoulder.

"I...came...to warn you!" he gasped as soon as he could catch his breath. "I overheard Dad say he saw you on TV last night. He said you got married." A grin broke over his face. "I think it's cool, but Dad's sure mad. Did you really get hitched?"

"No," Kelly answered. She glared at Max.

"Yes," Max answered. "That is, I think so. We were just—"

"I'll tell you later," Kelly interrupted with another urgent look over Sean's shoulder. "Come on in before Dad sees you."

Sean almost fell into the room. "Boy, is he going to be fried if he finds me here. Maybe I'd better go back home before he gets here."

Max stared at the boy who, in spite of his darker complexion, resembled Kelly. Her brother?

"No, you don't," a stern voice broke in. A uniformed officer of the Las Vegas Police Department filled the doorway.

Max thought rapidly. Had he broken some local

law last night? If the law was after him this afternoon, things must be worse than he thought.

"Patrick? Not you, too," Kelly squeaked.

Max took a closer look at the officer as the man grabbed Sean by a shoulder and hauled him into the room. He was a sturdy version of Kelly with the same hair color. Somehow, Max didn't care for the piercing look in his hazel eyes.

"Yeah, Patrick," the man agreed. "Your brother, remember?" He kept a grip on Sean who was trying to squirm out of his grasp. "As for you, kid, since you made it this far on your own, you might as well stay."

He scowled at Kelly. "For your information, the department's entire night shift congratulated me when I showed up for work this morning. Told me you got married on TV last night. Too bad you didn't let your own family in on your plans."

"Things aren't what they seem to be, honest," Kelly protested. "If you give me a minute, I can explain."

"What's to explain? From what I understand, you got married, period. Since I didn't even know you were seeing someone, let alone planning to marry him, I figured I'd better stop by and find out what's going on." He turned his solid gaze on Max. "You the groom?"

Momentarily overcome by the invasion of O'Rourkes, Max could only nod.

"I don't remember seeing you around," Patrick mused as he gave Max a thorough once-over. "New in town?"

Max shook his head and exchanged a dismayed

glance with Kelly. How many brothers did she have anyway? And what were they going to say if they knew the true state of affairs?

Kelly put her hands on her hips and glared at her brothers. "Max, these are two of my brothers, Sean and Patrick. Patrick is with the Las Vegas Police Department," she added as if it weren't obvious to Max. "He's the suspicious type. Sean's the youngest member of the family—he's fifteen."

Max had to give Kelly credit for keeping her cool under fire. Faced with the same situation, his sister would have probably fainted. He put down the telephone receiver and held out his hand. "The name is Maxwell Taylor. Er...I'm pleased to meet you."

"So, you're Kelly's husband." Patrick's features were impassive as he shook Max's hand, but his eyes spoke volumes. He was definitely not pleased.

"Kelly O'Rourke!" a new voice thundered. A tall man in an air force officer's uniform marched through the door. The man's crew-cut dark copper hair was fading into gray at the temples and his hazel eyes were grim. Max realized the newcomer had to be Kelly's father. He guessed trouble really did come in threes.

Behind Mr. O'Rourke was a younger man, also dressed in an air force uniform. Another brother? Max changed his opinion. Trouble came in as many numbers as there were O'Rourke men.

Surrounded by the power of the law and the military, Max's civilian heart took a dive. He tried to hide behind a smile.

"Dad, Damon?" Kelly pulled her robe more

closely around her. "What in heaven's name are all of you doing here at once?"

"A better question, Kelly O'Rourke," her father roared, "is what are *you* doing here!" Her father's bushy eyebrows rose in rebuke. "I understood you were going to be the maid of honor in DeeDee's wedding, but I didn't expect you to go so far as to get yourself married, too."

"I'm not— That is, I am, but—" Kelly caught herself and managed a feeble smile. "That is, it was sort of a surprise to me, too." She sent a quick, pleading glance at Max.

"Is this your young man?"

Max felt he was about to undergo an interrogation. Too bad he had no ready answers. He couldn't tell the unvarnished truth, not with the silent appeal in Kelly's eyes. He held out his hand to have it grasped in a firm handshake he was going to feel for a week. "Maxwell Taylor, sir."

"Michael O'Rourke. Glad to meet you, my boy," Kelly's father answered with a final shake. He regarded Max through narrowed eyes. "Not that I'm all too happy over my daughter's elopement, you understand. But considering her impulsive nature, I suppose I shouldn't have been too surprised." He gazed reprovingly at Sean. "This young one here seems to have the same knack for doing the unexpected, but I think I have time to cure that."

Kelly gasped. "Dad, how can you say such things?"

"The proof is standing next to you," her father answered, gesturing to Max. "So, what do the two of you have to say for yourselves?"

Max took a quick inventory of his chances with this audience and shot Kelly a warning glance.

Damon, an air force officer like his father. Patrick, a local Las Vegas lawman. All three highly trained with instincts and senses honed to a razor's edge. All sharp and unlikely to be fooled easily. On the other hand, there was Sean. From the boy's sheepish grin, Max sensed Sean was a maverick like his sister.

At least there was one friendly male member of the O'Rourke clan.

Max caught Patrick's frown as he stared at Kelly, almost as if he were on a criminal case. Max's own gaze followed Patrick's to the hand Kelly used to clutch the robe to her throat. To his mind the answer to Patrick's frown was clear. Kelly, ostensibly a newly married woman, wasn't wearing a wedding ring.

Max stirred himself. The moment of truth was at hand. Husband or not, for Kelly's sake, if not his own, he owed her his support. "Here, sweetheart, let me help you with that," he said. On the pretext of helping her close the bathrobe more closely around her neck, he managed to slip his class ring off his finger and onto Kelly's wedding-ring finger. With a warning look into her startled eyes, he turned back to the O'Rourkes. Just in time to glimpse a shadow cross Patrick's face. Moments later, he saw Patrick's gaze settle on the bridal bouquet and the wedding veil on the coffee table.

Max responded to the stunned look on Kelly's face. He had to do something to break the tension before Patrick started asking questions for which he and

Kelly had no answers. The sooner the better. "Sweetheart, why don't you go in and get dressed?"

She nodded reluctantly. "Okay. I'll be back in a minute, Dad. Max, can I see you in the other room for a moment?"

"Sure," Max answered. Before he followed Kelly, he noticed the envious look in Sean's eyes as the boy studied the untouched champagne breakfast. "Sean, why don't you help yourself to some breakfast? No use letting it go to waste."

Kelly pulled Max into the bedroom and pushed the folding doors together. She pointed to the open slats on the doors, then dragged him into the bathroom and carefully closed the door behind her. Soft, romantic music filtered through the room. "What in heaven's name are we going to do now?"

"Good question." Max gazed at the exotic surroundings that were obviously designed to stir a man's senses. Even with trouble waiting for him in the other room, his thoughts turned to putting the scented oils to good use. He blinked. Of all the fool times to think sensuous thoughts, this was probably the worst.

"Brazen it out, I guess," he answered, firmly turning his thoughts to the more serious issue at hand. "We'll just pretend everything is okay until they leave. Then, if it turns out we actually were married last night, we can talk about an annulment."

"An annulment? After last night?" Her startled expression got through to Max. She was right. Married or not, they *had* shared an intimate night together. An annulment was probably out.

"Okay, maybe not an annulment," he answered. "Maybe a divorce."

"That's ridiculous," Kelly muttered angrily. "In the first place, I keep telling you we're not married. In the second, O'Rourkes don't get divorced! That's why neither of my older brothers are married—they're waiting for the right woman. As for my getting a divorce, it's out of the question. I'd be breaking Dad's heart!"

"Keep it down," Max cautioned. "This is what I think we ought to do. For now, we'll tell your family we're going on a honeymoon. We can settle all this later when we're alone."

"Honeymoon?" Looking outraged, Kelly demanded, "Honeymoon? Who said anything about a honeymoon?"

"Take it easy, Kelly," he soothed, with one eye on the bathroom door. If they didn't come to some sort of agreement soon, he expected an O'Rourke to be pounding on the door in minutes. "It'll only be a pretend honeymoon. Just long enough to get your family off our backs."

"Maybe." She didn't look mollified, but she finally agreed. "But don't let Patrick fool you. Damon, either. If you knew them as well as I do, you'd know they're up to something."

"Now you're being paranoid," Max answered, his nerves shot. "You're their sister. It's natural to worry about you."

"That's the problem. They think they have to keep an eye on me. It drives me crazy. There were times when I was a kid that I used to think my thoughts

were engraved on my forehead.'' She rubbed her forehead. ''I sure hope this isn't one of those times.''

With a last regretful glance at the Jacuzzi, Max
turned Kelly toward the mirror. ''Take a look. There's
nothing written on your forehead. Besides, as a married woman, you don't have to account to your brothers.''

Instead of continuing to argue, Kelly looked into
the mirror. Max's hands held her by the shoulders,
his chin rested on her hair. He was right. Except for
a frown, her forehead was clear. But, to her chagrin,
there was definitely an awareness of Max reflected in
her eyes. As her gaze met his in the mirror, she read
the same awareness in his. The strange excitement she
remembered beginning with the garter ceremony began to fill her again.

''We aren't really married, you know,'' she murmured. She was strangely unwilling to break the sensual tension between them, but the truth was the truth.

''Why don't we wait and see,'' he said softly as he
drew a damp tendril from her forehead. ''In the meantime, we're in this together.''

''Thank you,'' she answered gratefully. ''But I'm
not sure we'll hear the last of this. Even if Dad's
convinced we're married, I know he's disappointed.
He would have preferred a traditional Irish church
wedding with all the O'Rourkes in attendance.'' She
worried her bottom lip. ''We'll have to be careful. In
the meantime, please go along with whatever my dad
says until we're alone. Okay?''

Max had a gut feeling she was right. He felt guilty,
although he wasn't quite sure why. Having too much
punch? Becoming attracted to Kelly and marrying her

on impulse? Consummating their wedding night? Any or all of the above?

He couldn't afford to dwell on the possibilities, not now. Not when judgment day waited for him as near as the next room.

What further complicated the situation in his mind was that they were obviously on Kelly's home territory, or her father and brothers wouldn't have shown up so soon. With his own home and his family in the East, he had little to lose. He also had a plane ticket to Hawaii in his suitcase for a few days from now. He'd intended to spend some time in Vegas and enjoy the nightlife, then fly on to Hawaii for a much-needed vacation with Lian. Left behind, Kelly, for all her bravado, was the vulnerable one. The least he could do for her was to find out what really happened last night and to make sure she wouldn't get hurt. Not by himself, or anyone else. And that went for her father and her brothers, too.

"Why don't you get dressed?" he said. "We'll work something out when you come back in. Okay?"

One thing he was sure of, Max resolved as he left Kelly to dress, for her sake there couldn't be any talk of an annulment or divorce with her family around. Pretending he was a loving new groom when he had to keep his distance from the most attractive woman he'd ever met was going to be a hell of a way to spend his vacation.

Sean was deep in croissants and jam when Max walked back into the living room. To Max's further dismay, Damon was gazing at the bridal bouquet with a frown on his face. Patrick, involved in conversation with his father, looked up when Max walked in.

"Kelly?" Patrick asked.

"She'll be out in a few minutes." Before Max could say anything more, a knock on the door sounded a reprieve.

With a wry shrug, Max opened the door. "Your coffee, Mr. Taylor." The room-service waiter rolled in a small cart. "Anything else?"

A miracle. "No thanks, that'll be all." He reached into his pocket for his wallet. "It's on the house, Mr. Taylor," the waiter said, smiling and backing out the door. "Comes with the bridal suite. Congratulations."

Max's heart sank. He'd never be able to talk his way out of this mess. Not with strangers congratulating him on a marriage he could scarcely remember.

Kelly's father took the cup of coffee Max offered. The questions Max expected came as swiftly as a hail of bullets. "Since I've not seen you around here, I was wondering where you come from. What do you do for a living? And how and where you met Kelly? Have you known each other long?"

Michael O'Rourke was obviously no fool, but a quick glance at the expression on Patrick's face was all Max needed to realize where the questions had come from. He'd been around the law often enough to recognize official questions when he heard them.

"Long enough to know I wanted Kelly for my wife," Max answered briskly. "I live in Boston. I have my own business of fitness centers. As for when I met Kelly, I saw her a few times when I visited Troy, and she and DeeDee came over. Anything else?"

"Not at the moment. But let me tell you that I would have expected you to have taken the time to ask me for my daughter's hand before you decided to get married. Or at least invited her family to the wedding."

"I suppose you could say it was a spur-of-the-moment decision, Mr. O'Rourke," Max answered truthfully. "We couldn't seem to help ourselves."

"'Mr. O'Rourke?' What's the matter with calling me Dad now that you've married my daughter?" Kelly's father sighed. "I suppose times have changed from when I was a young man and asked for my Moira's hand." He sighed again. "Naturally, I would have preferred to give my only daughter away at a proper church wedding with her family in attendance." He gazed reprovingly at Max. "I hate to think of what her sainted mother would say about all of this." His eyes narrowed. "Still, if we do this properly, it may not be too late."

Cold shivers danced on Max's spine at the realization that the marriage game was becoming more complicated as the minutes flew by.

"You both will have to come home with me for a few days," his new father-in-law announced. "You can meet Kelly's extended family and give them all a chance to get to know you."

Before Max could protest, Kelly appeared in the doorway wearing her crumpled maid-of-honor gown and holding a hairbrush in her hand. "We'll have to do what?"

"Come home and let your husband meet the rest of the family," her father repeated. "As I told him, it's not too late."

"Too late for what?" Kelly demanded. Eye to eye,

toe to toe, green eyes blazing, she challenged her father.

"A proper church wedding!"

From the tone in his voice, Max could tell Michael O'Rourke wasn't used to being challenged, not from anyone, least of all his daughter. When the man's eyebrows rose to new heights, Max could feel big trouble brewing.

Kelly's face became as flushed as her father's. "We're already married, Dad!" She gestured to the festive gown she wore. "You said yourself you saw us getting married on television last night."

Max snapped to attention. She'd spent the last few hours protesting he was crazy, insisting they weren't married. *Now* she was changing her mind?

"True, but there's still a matter of a proper wedding," her father answered firmly. In the background, Damon and Patrick murmured their agreement. Sean grinned his sympathy and shrugged his shoulders. Max sensed the kid had wisely elected to keep his opinions to himself.

"Max, say something!" Kelly's voice drew Max back into the argument.

"Maybe a visit can wait for later on," Max answered. He took Kelly's hand in his and squeezed it gently in a silent warning. "To tell the truth, Mr. O'Rourke, I'm on a short vacation. Time for our honeymoon is limited."

"Maybe so," Kelly's father answered, "but there's still the family to consider and your future plans to discuss. In any case, I still expect you both to spend a day or two under my roof so everyone can meet you. We'll use the base dining hall and have a big party. The military is like an extended family, so we'll invite them too. For Kelly's sake, since she works there,'' he added meaningfully.

"But, Dad—"

"No buts, Kelly O'Rourke! My mind is made up. I'll expect both of you tonight!"

Max put his arm around a protesting Kelly and, under the pretext of kissing her ear, whispered, "Agree with him. We'll think of something later on."

"You have no idea what you're letting yourself in for," Kelly whispered, matching her father's glare over Max's shoulder.

"I'm sure everything is going to be okay," Max answered. What he didn't tell Kelly was he was aware that in an obviously traditional family setting such as the O'Rourkes' appeared to be, and his own, for that matter, a free-spirited woman like Kelly, and her name, needed all the protection she could get.

He turned back to the man who had just become his father-in-law. "We'll be along directly, Mr. O'Rourke."

"Don't be long," the senior O'Rourke warned. "We'll expect you before sundown. Come on, boys."

As soon as the door closed behind her family, a distraught Kelly turned on Max. "You don't really expect us to spend the night at my house, do you?"

"I'm afraid we have to."

"Instead of giving in to my father's wishes, why aren't you out trying to find a wedding license or a marriage certificate?"

"I've been trying to ever since I woke up. It's been one damn thing after another. And now your family shows up. I haven't had a moment's peace today, so don't you start.'' Max headed for the room-service cart. "Coffee?"

"No, thanks.'' Kelly paced to the window and stared out at the busy Las Vegas thoroughfare. "There ought to be something we can do."

"I'll go to the marriage-license bureau first thing tomorrow morning and check the records.'' Max reached for a blueberry muffin. "Are you sure you don't want something to eat?"

"The way I feel, I don't think I could handle anything. You go ahead and eat if you want to,'' Kelly answered without looking back.

"Suit yourself,'' Max said. "I'm going to get cleaned up before we head out to your place. In the meantime, you might practice being a wife."

"Practice being a wife?" Obviously affronted, Kelly swung around. "I don't intend to *be* a wife at all.'' With her squared jaw and set lips, Max was inclined to believe she meant what she said. Not that it mattered. As his mother often said, they'd made their bed and they had to lie in it. This time—worse luck—platonically.

Chapter Three

No one was home to welcome Max and Kelly when they reported to the O'Rourke residence on Nellis Air Force Base. Max was relieved. Maybe he and Kelly would finally find time to plan their next move. Then, tomorrow, he intended to head over to the marriage-license bureau and do some checking.

Things might have been different, even desirable, if he and Kelly cared for each other. Instead, circumstances forced them to pretend they were madly in love. Sure, they *were* attracted to each other, but so far they couldn't seem to carry on a sensible conversation without winding up in an argument.

As he followed Kelly into the bedroom, he took heart in knowing they would soon go their separate ways. All he needed to do was persuade Kelly's father he intended to take her on a honeymoon. With a little luck, he'd be a free man by tomorrow night.

Her bedroom reminded him of his dorm room back at college. The bed, covered by a patchwork quilt, was pushed against one wall. A small maple desk and chair, an ancient leather lounge chair and a reading lamp were positioned under a window. A matching maple chest of drawers crowded a corner. There were plenty of homey touches—family photographs on the walls, two heart-shaped pillows, a hand-hooked rug.

Max wasn't surprised. In his experience, a woman's bedroom reflected her personality. Under that sexy exterior he'd encountered last night, he had an uneasy feeling Kelly was a hometown, traditional woman. The kind that wanted to nest. Thank goodness she apparently didn't want to nest with him.

He gazed doubtfully at Kelly's single bed. The bed might do for a woman her size, but it didn't look big enough to accommodate the addition of a six-foot-two-inch, one-hundred-and-eighty-five-pound man. Sharing the narrow bed wasn't going to be easy. The worn beige and brown leather chair didn't look very inviting as an alternative, either. He was beginning to understand what Kelly meant when she'd told him he didn't know what he was letting himself in for.

"Not exactly a palace, is it?" he asked.

"No, it's not," Kelly agreed. She glanced around the room and shrugged. "You can't say I didn't try to warn you."

"I thought you were talking about your father," Max protested. "I figured I could handle him later. Sleeping in a bed that size with you wasn't exactly what I was expecting." He gazed at the bed with a jaundiced air. "Maybe I can change your father's mind when he comes home."

"Fat chance," Kelly answered wearily. "I've never been able to change it once he's made up his mind."

"Come on, Kelly. Don't blame it all on your father. You're the one who insisted we were married."

"Maybe so," she agreed, "but since it was pretty obvious we'd slept together, I said we were married to keep him from taking a shotgun to you. Besides, from the way Patrick was eyeing you, I was afraid he'd haul you off to jail if I hadn't jumped in to stop him."

"Jail? Be serious. For sleeping with you?" Max swallowed a grin when Kelly blushed. Maybe he shouldn't have been so blunt, but it seemed to him, if ever there was a time to call a spade a spade, this was it. Married or not, they *had* slept together. As far as he knew, it wasn't a local offense.

"No, for vagrancy, or some other charge." Kelly bit back a rueful smile. "My brother Patrick thinks like a policeman. After he took a good look at you, I could tell he was looking for a chance to run you in."

Max looked down at his navy-blue tailored pants and blazer, shirt and tie. "What's wrong with the way I look?"

"That's easy." Kelly held up her left hand and counted off on her fingers. "You're obviously not Irish, in the military or on the police force. I'm sure Patrick will come up with a few more reasons as soon as he's had a chance to check you out."

Max began to believe he'd somehow wandered into a special place peopled by a tribe of weird O'Rourkes. "Who in heaven's name made up rules like that?"

"Dad," she answered succinctly. She tossed the bouquet and bridal veil on the desk. "He's been preaching those rules to me ever since I had my first date. And *that* was with either Damon or Patrick and their dates in tow. I was lucky Dad didn't insist on coming along, too."

Max bridled. "What's the matter with someone like me for a husband? I'm not exactly a bum." He pumped up his chest. "I'll have you know I own Taylor Fitness Centers."

"The gyms?" As Kelly asked, she recalled DeeDee telling her when she'd regaled Kelly with Max's attributes. "We're a great match, then. I teach aerobics on the base." She shrugged. "But as long as you aren't Irish, I'm afraid you're not on Dad's list of eligible males."

The thought that he could end up in jail, even for twenty-four hours while Patrick checked him out, struck Max as ridiculous.

About as ridiculous as the entire situation. The more he thought about it, the more he didn't know what to believe.

He raked his fingers through his hair and stared at Kelly.

What he *was* beginning to believe was that Kelly represented everything he was beginning to feel was missing in his life; spontaneity, independence, dynamism, fun. And that he was more attracted to her than he'd realized.

To complicate matters, without a wedding license or marriage certificate, he couldn't be sure of anything, let alone his own sanity.

Kelly sighed her exasperation. "I told my father we were married to get him off your back, and sure, I wanted him off mine too. I'm not worried about Dad. I think he's willing to believe me. It's the way Patrick and Damon looked that worries me."

"As a matter of fact, me too." Max looked around for a place to stash his suitcase, but there didn't seem to be an empty place. "Especially when I caught Patrick looking for your wedding ring. Maybe I ought to go out and buy you a ring before your father gets back."

"Don't bother." Kelly dropped onto the bed, kicked off her shoes and peeled off her silk stockings. "We only have tonight to worry about." She frowned at the bridal veil. "What am I doing with DeeDee's bridal veil?"

Max tried to clear the cobwebs from his mind. "Beats me. Maybe she loaned it to you when we got married."

"Don't be ridiculous," Kelly scoffed. "In spite of what I told my father, we're not married. Never have been, never will be. I remember almost everything that happened last night and applying for a wedding license wasn't one of them. So, in spite of what happened last night, we couldn't possibly be married."

"In that case, I guess I'm out of here," Max responded with a twinge of regret that surprised him. "I'm not looking forward to being your brother Patrick's target." Max hoisted his suitcase. "Well?"

Kelly sat up with a look of alarm. "You can't leave now! I need you to back up my story!"

"Some story," Max muttered. "Just remember, you can't have it both ways. Either we're married, or we're not."

"Just for tonight, Max. Please?"

Max felt a pang of sympathy at the near panic in her voice. There *was* that growing attraction he felt for her. And her reputation with the family was shaky, at best. "Okay. But if you keep changing your mind, no one is going to believe you. Including me."

He looked around for a place to put his suitcase. "I don't know about you, but it's beginning to look to me as if we're in a hole so deep, we're never going to be able to dig our way out." *Do you really want to?* Where had that thought come from?

He tore his gaze from Kelly's slender right leg that had caused all his trouble. "Er...I'm sure that bed is too small for the two of us. Maybe we can try for some other sleeping arrangements?"

Kelly looked around her bedroom, then shrugged. "I doubt it. I don't think Dad would let us get away with not staying here tonight, or with your sleeping on the couch. It would be a dead giveaway. I know the house isn't very big, but it's been home for the last year for Dad, Sean and me."

"Your brothers?"

"Damon lives in the bachelor-officers' quarters. Patrick has an apartment in Las Vegas, but they're in and out all the time. They'll probably show up later."

Max sighed. "Okay. Just for tonight. Where can I stash my suitcase?"

"I'm afraid you'll have to try under the bed. The closet is full."

Max contemplated the logistics of sliding his suitcase under the bed with Kelly's hips inches away from his eyes. The spicy fragrance surrounding her reminded him of the exotic bathroom at the Majestic Hotel. The effect the scent had had on him was back, big time.

He studied the bed one more time. It looked as if a platonic night was going to be shaky. "How do you expect me to..." He caught himself before he asked the burning question that was bothering him. How was he going to keep his hands off Kelly if they had to share that bed? He fought the urge to turn on his heel and make tracks.

"Expect you to do what?"

He felt himself flush. But what the heck, they had to face facts sooner or later. "I meant to ask, how do you expect both of us to manage with such a small bed?"

Before Kelly could answer, a small furry bundle raced into the room. The dog ran past a startled Max, jumped into Kelly's arms and licked her face furiously.

Max backed away before the animal came at him. Kelly's attention last night had been welcome, but canine kisses weren't his idea of affection. "Yours?"

"Mine," Kelly agreed happily. She hugged the wiggling cocker spaniel. "Her name is Honey."

Max was bemused at the airy kisses Kelly showered on the little animal. "I've never had a pet of my own. We weren't allowed to have pets at boarding school."

"You don't know what you're missing." Kelly laughed happily and returned the dog's frantic kisses. "I left her with the family next door yesterday. She must have come in the doggie door." Another hug. "Honey is my best friend. We move so often, everything and everyone else seems to have passed through my life like a moving train."

"That must have been hard on you." Max studied Kelly thoughtfully, aware of her for the first time as a person instead of only as a desirable woman. No wonder she needed someone like Honey in her life. As for himself, where would he fit in? "My family has lived in the same house in Boston for generations.''

''You're lucky. We've lived in places like this all over the world. That's part of the reason I got into teaching aerobics. It's flexible. Anyway, if you're a military brat, you have to get used to being a loner. As for a residence, every house and every bedroom on every air force base looks like this one.''

Max heard the unhappiness in Kelly's voice. His own life was predictable, scheduled to a gnat's eyebrow on a strict agenda—even as a child. What would it be like to be uprooted from schools and friends every few years?

''Ever think of busting loose?'' he asked tentatively.

''Sometimes,'' she answered wistfully. ''Especially whenever I thought Dad and my older brothers were unreasonable and too controlling.'' She buried her head in Honey's fur and crooned softly.

Max felt a pang of envy as the dog licked Kelly's nose. Maybe Kelly's background was the answer to last night. Had it been a time she had decided to cut loose, to make love with a man of her own choice? Or did she really care for him? Strangely enough, he was beginning to wish she did.

Kelly set the dog on a heart-shaped pillow. ''Sit!'' When the dog obediently froze, Kelly smiled at her pet approvingly. She gazed down at her bridesmaid's gown. ''I'm beginning to feel as if this dress has been glued to me. I've got to change.'' She rummaged in the small chest and came up with jeans and a dark green plaid woolen shirt.

Glued to her was right, Max mused. The velvet

dress clung to her curves as if it had been sewn on. He cleared his throat. "Go ahead. I'll just get rid of this thing." He bent to stow his suitcase under the bed but retreated at Honey's low growl. "Okay, have it your way," he muttered, "but you're going to have to let me get near that bed sooner or later." He'd be damned if he'd get into a territorial dispute with a dog.

With a smile he hoped Honey would interpret as friendly, Max studied an O'Rourke family picture hanging on the wall. Her father was dressed in a military uniform with a lieutenant's insignia on its shoulders. A sweet-faced, dark-haired woman, Damon and Patrick, serious even at a young age, stood at her side. A smiling young Kelly and a small dark-haired boy sat on the floor in front of them. "The woman in this picture—your mother?"

"Yes," Kelly emerged from the closet with a pair of sport shoes. "We lost her about five years ago."

"Sorry," Max answered. "That must have been rough." His gaze swung to the faded heart-shaped pillows, the handmade quilt that was on Kelly's bed and hooked rug. They'd probably been made by her mother and kept close no matter how many times the family had moved. Under Kelly's feisty bravado obviously beat a sentimental heart.

"Mostly on Sean, I guess, since he was so young. He and I have always been close. Since I was the only woman around, I guess you could say I helped raise him."

"The kid seems to have turned out okay. I'd say you did a good job."

"Thank you." Kelly laughed. "It's always been

the two of us against Dad and my other brothers—
we're different. Dad wants Sean to be more like Damon and Patrick, to go into the military or law en-
forcement. Or almost any career that requires a
uniform. Dad insists public service is character-
building. Poor Sean, he's not the type. He'd rather
study computer animation when he gets out of high
school. He'll do it, too. He's a born rebel.''

"Like you?"

"I guess so.'' She laughed again. ''But he's
quicker on his feet and in his head than I ever was.
With three controlling males in my life, I couldn't get
away with anything.'' She disappeared through the
bathroom door, but not before she shot him a dazzling
smile. ''Maybe now that I'm married, things will be
different.''

Married? Was she kidding—or did she honestly believe they were married? Max was totally bewildered.
About the only thing he was certain of was how impossible it would be to share a bed with her and still
keep his hands to himself.

Through the closed bathroom door, he heard Kelly
muttering her frustration.

"Need some help?"

"Not unless you can undo buttons with your eyes
closed.''

Max swallowed his grin. ''Come on, Kelly, we
shared a great deal more than buttons last night. So,
what would be the problem if I saw your back now?''

"The problem is, Maxwell Taylor,'' she called, ''I
don't think either of us was responsible for what we
did last night. But if you hadn't started flirting, or if
the champagne punch hadn't been so strong, I would

have made it through the night okay. What was your excuse?''

Max thought for a long moment. How could he tell her he'd been so taken by her saucy smile, he'd deliberately flirted with her? Or that he'd worked until nine o'clock the Friday night before the wedding and had caught a red-eye into Las Vegas. The end result had been to leave him half-awake and vulnerable to the same champagne punch she'd complained about. ''I'm afraid I don't have a good excuse, unless you're willing to accept I was suffering from jet lag.''

''Yeah, sure. Ouch!''

Max swung around. ''What's wrong?''

''Darn. I've caught my hair in one of the buttons.''

''Come on out here,'' Max coaxed, turning his thoughts to a more platonic problem than his growing attraction for Kelly. ''This sounds like a real emergency.''

''It sure is.'' Her hair caught on a button, Kelly slowly backed her way out of the bathroom.

Under Honey's watchful eyes, Max gingerly untangled the tangled lock of red hair. Her scent, the silken feel of her soft skin, turned his thoughts back to the moment he'd awakened that afternoon and found her sleeping beside him.

Buttons be damned. What he wanted was to taste her lips again, fold her in his arms again, and bring last night's memories to life. And maybe even to consider the possibility of a future with her.

Where are these thoughts coming from? he asked himself. He didn't know, but suddenly he didn't feel the need to examine their origin anymore.

He slowly undid the remaining velvet buttons on Kelly's dress, lingering longer than he should have.

"Max?"

Max took a deep breath to clear his head. "In a minute." With Kelly's strong appeal, her winning smile and yes, even her flashes of Irish temper, he was afraid he was in deeper than he'd intended to be. If this kept up, he was going to wind up being married to Kelly for real. Damn! He had to find that license or certificate soon or he'd go out of his mind.

Out of the corner of his eye he noted Honey's watchful eyes. With Kelly's lock of hair finally untangled, he stepped back. "Maybe I ought to wait outside while you finish changing. We can make our plans later."

Kelly blinked. "What plans?"

"For our honeymoon."

Holding her dress to keep it from falling, Kelly stopped in midstride on her way back to the bathroom. "What honeymoon?" she said over her shoulder as she entered the bathroom and shut the door.

"The one I told your father we planned on taking."

"You're serious, aren't you?"

"Of course I am. I told you, talking to your father about a honeymoon is the only way I can think of for us to get out of this mess. Once we're out of here, you can go your way and I'll go mine. That is, if you still want out." He was beginning to hope she didn't.

"You may be right," Kelly agreed, but Max could tell he was on the right track. This might be Kelly's only chance to go off on her own, but she didn't sound as convinced she wanted to cut loose as she had earlier. "But what about the wedding Dad's planning?"

"I'll speak to him about our wedding, as one man to another. I'll try to make him understand any legal wedding makes a marriage. Even if it isn't the kind he would have chosen for you. The important thing is to get him to back off and leave us alone so we can make our own decisions."

"Without a wedding license or a marriage certificate, good luck on proving ours was a legal marriage," Kelly muttered. "And the way Patrick was looking at us, that's the next thing he's going to ask for. Whatever you thought happened last night, I'd be surprised if you find one."

"Maybe you'll be surprised," Max answered. As Honey scratched at her collar, he ran his finger around his neckline to loosen his own collar that had suddenly grown uncomfortably tight. "I've heard getting married in Las Vegas is easy, so I don't expect your brothers will give us a lot of static about the way we went about ours."

"You don't know my brothers," Kelly said soundly as she entered the bedroom, fully dressed.

"Maybe not, but I haven't given up looking for proof we were married. I intend to keep at it. In the meantime, I suggest we insist on a honeymoon. Like I said, once we're out of sight, you can go your way and I can go mine."

Kelly blinked at the sudden change in Max's voice. She'd sensed his earlier physical reaction to her when she'd come out of the bathroom with one shoulder bare. She'd felt his desire radiate over her when he'd stood behind her to loosen her hair. She'd felt it so strongly, her own body had caught fire. What had caused the change in him? Was the charade almost over?

The problem was she remembered too much about last night. His searching hands, his warm breath against her breasts, the taste of his lips on hers. She remembered only too well his hard strong body finally joining hers and the burst of pleasure that had claimed her. She could have left anytime after Max had fallen asleep, but there had been something about him that had called her to stay. By the time she'd awakened again, it had been too late to leave.

Still, Max was probably more right about their situation than she cared to admit. She'd told her father she and Max were married, not only to forestall an argument, but to gain her freedom. She had to let the memories go, to look forward to making a new life for herself.

Honey jumped off the bed, scampered over to Max and started to growl.

Max backed away. "What's wrong with the mutt?"

Kelly picked up the dog and crooned reassuringly in its ear. "The tone of your voice must have spooked her. Or maybe she thinks I'm going to leave her again."

Max regarded Honey, quiet now but still wary. "Does she understand human speech?"

Kelly giggled at the incredulous look on Max's face. "Dogs are more human than most people realize. It was probably your body language that spooked her."

"That's all I need, another watchdog," Max muttered. "Patrick is enough. I hope you don't intend to take her with you on our honeymoon."

"If there is a honeymoon," Kelly replied. "Either way, where I go, she goes."

"Of all the fool ideas I've ever heard, that one was the worst," a male voice roared. The fiberboard walls of the house seemed to shake with the man's anger. Kelly held her breath and went out to meet her father. Max followed in time to see Michael O'Rourke storm into the house followed by Patrick and Damon. Sean trailed behind them and winked at Kelly and Max.

"Something wrong, Dad?" Kelly said.

Kelly's father turned his angry gaze on Kelly. "Stupid is more like it!"

From her father's accusing look, Kelly instinctively knew she and Max were involved. "What's the problem?"

"The problem is the base chaplain refuses to marry you and Max. Father Joe insists the two of you need to know each other better before he'll marry you."

"But, Dad, I told you Max and I are already married!"

"An elopement in a Las Vegas hotel?" her father snorted. "That was no marriage. When I asked Joe to perform a real wedding in the base chapel, the fool refused. He wants to wait until he has a chance to meet and counsel the two of you to be sure it's not a classic case of marry in haste and repent at leisure."

With a cautionary glance at Max, Kelly moved closer to him. "That's okay with us, but later, please. I insist on a honeymoon now. Max has to go back to work."

Behind her, Max stirred. "Let me handle this, Kelly."

"No!" Kelly glared at Max. "I'm tired of being told what to do. It's my life! *I* say we're going on a honeymoon. Starting tomorrow morning."

"Now see here, Kelly," her father growled. He shook a finger at her. "You're putting the cart before the horse. You have to get married properly before you go off on a honeymoon. After all, there might be consequences." His eyes blazed beneath his bushy eyebrows.

Consequences? No way, Max reassured himself. When he'd changed out of his tuxedo back at the hotel, he remembered checking his wallet for the protection he usually carried. To his relief, he'd come up empty.

On the other hand, maybe he'd jumped to the wrong conclusion too fast.

There *had* been a deep, satisfied feeling of peace when he'd awakened this afternoon with Kelly's creamy shoulder up against his bare chest. Judging from the contented smile on her face and the condition of the bed they had been in, the night must have been filled with more than pleasant erotic dreams.

Definitely, once hadn't been enough.

Max felt his stomach begin to churn.

Maybe it was a good thing he was so sure he and Kelly were married.

At the rate the argument between Kelly and her father was going, and at the accusing looks Patrick and Damon were sending him, Max realized the red-headed O'Rourkes were too stubborn to compromise easily. He was a stranger, a civilian, definitely not

Irish and, according to Kelly, therefore suspect. Still it was up to him to do something before things got out of hand. Before he jumped into the fray, he tightened his arms around Kelly in warning.

Kelly's father glanced at Sean's grinning face. "This isn't the time nor the place for this discussion. We'll talk about this later."

Kelly mentally crossed her fingers and backed into Max's arms. "I think you're wrong, Dad, but that's okay, too. One wedding is good enough for me."

"Well, it's not good enough for me," her father replied. He regarded Max with deep suspicion before he gave in. "However, since I'm sure no reputable minister or priest around here will marry you if the word gets out about Joe turning me down, I'm willing to compromise. I'll rent you a houseboat for the honeymoon. That way, you'll be close enough to come back and meet the family. If you agree, I'll go along with a short delay. What do you say?"

Max thought about it. "How long are you talking about?"

"A week."

Kelly gasped. "No way!"

Max held her closer. She might be feisty, a stubborn redhead like her father, but he still felt her tremble in his arms. His respect for her grew, and so did his determination to protect her. But he could see there was no way he could sway her father without creating a hell for all concerned.

He eyed his father-in-law. "You're right. We accept. As long as we can leave tomorrow morning."

Chapter Four

"Max Taylor, is there something wrong with you?" Kelly erupted when the last of the O'Rourke men disappeared. "Why did you agree to this houseboat honeymoon? There's just so much of this nonsense I can take." She pulled out of Max's arms and headed back to her bedroom.

Max stopped long enough to shake off Honey's firm grip on his trouser leg before he followed her. "I'm afraid there might be a problem."

Kelly pulled to a stop and Max ran into her. Momentum carried them onto the bed in a tangle of arms and legs. Instinctively, Max bent to take her lips in his.

Kelly's lips tasted as sweet as honey and stirred hazy memories. Memories of last night when Kelly had been warm and willing. A night when he had believed she was his wife.

Lost in her instinctive response tonight, Max ignored the voice at the back of his consciousness that whispered caution. In spite of that voice, tonight Kelly *was* his wife.

Caught unawares, Kelly found herself returning his

embrace. If this was going to be their last night together, she wanted to share every moment of it with him before the time came for them to part.

"Another problem?" Kelly asked breathlessly when she managed to catch her breath. She lay gazing up at Max. "What new problem are you talking about?"

Max sat up and took a deep breath. Controlling himself wasn't easy, but he owed it to Kelly to be truthful. "I'll tell you in a minute. But first I want you to take it easy. Try to remember I'm on your side, okay?" Kelly nodded. "To be honest," he went on with a wary eye on her, "there *is* a chance your father could be right."

"Right about what?"

"About possible consequences—a baby." At the dark look that came into Kelly's eyes, Max stood up and cautiously took a step backward.

"Which baby are we talking about?" The tone of her voice boded no good.

Max knew he had to be up-front with Kelly—there was no use beating around the bush. After all, he'd been raised to believe telling the truth could never hurt him. From the ominous tone in Kelly's voice, he wasn't too sure the adage applied to the present case. Still, her father had raised a question that needed addressing. "Ours."

Kelly's hazel eyes darkened. Her jaw squared and she pulled herself up. "*Our* baby? No way! I distinctly remember you saying you used protection."

"I did. But it was a long night and you were so appealing and I was…" He stopped when he realized he was babbling. "Anyway, I swear I thought we were married."

Kelly's protest died in her throat as mental images of last night came to mind. A night when Max's appeal had been so strong she hadn't been able to get enough of him. Nor, from the sensual details she remembered with a blush, had he been able to get enough of her. An attraction that, even under the circumstances, still seemed to arc between them.

She recalled the raspy feel of his naked chest against hers, the salty taste of his skin against her lips. The tiny love bites, the deep mind-boggling kisses, the sound of his voice murmuring love words into her ear. The night had been long, full of loving and unforgettable. Max might profess not to be too clear about last night, but *she* remembered the important parts—too well for her own peace of mind.

Married or not, once hadn't been enough last night.

"Are you sure?" she asked, her mind going in a dozen directions when he nodded.

It wasn't that she didn't love and want children of her own, but this was hardly the time to begin motherhood. Not until she and Max could find the proof they were actually husband and wife.

Besides, her goal had been to rid herself of the men in her life for now, not to acquire a new one. Especially one she hardly knew—except in a biblical sense.

She'd been taught to believe a husband and wife were blessed when they married. That when children came, they were doubly blessed. And that marriage definitely came first.

"Maybe you were wrong about last night," she

said hopefully. He wasn't smiling. "So, how do you feel about babies?" Her question was tentative, but she held her breath waiting for his answer.

"They're okay, I guess. It's just that this isn't the most convenient time for one, is it?"

She had to agree with him there. "No, I guess not."

She gazed down at her narrow bed, envisioned the two of them trying to sleep there together. Clearly, under the circumstances, sleep was going to be impossible. "Now what?"

"I think we should go along with your father. Let's stick it out together for a while. At least through the honeymoon. What do you think?"

"I thought we'd agreed to go our separate ways as soon as possible, but you're still talking about going on a honeymoon?"

"Of course. It's the only way we can manage to find a way to get lost without your family breathing down our necks."

"Hah." Kelly sniffed her indifference, but Max wasn't buying. She looked as troubled about her father's reaction to their marriage and possible baby as he was.

"Look," he said. "We don't know if there *is* going to be a baby. Why don't we wait until you're sure?"

"I'm not worried," she lied. She was. A child needed a willing father and mother. She mentally crossed her fingers. "As for getting lost, if I know Patrick and his playmates," she went on, "we'd have to honeymoon in the middle of the Sahara to be by ourselves. And even then, Patrick would probably find us."

"Don't be too sure," Max answered. "I think your father has come up with a honeymoon that will solve the problem. No," he said as she started to protest again, "we can talk about it later. I'm tired. And if you expect us to share this bed of yours, you'll have to do something about that mutt." He glanced at the heart-shaped pillows where Honey crouched, panting her unhappiness. "There's not enough room in there for the three of us."

Kelly blew Honey a kiss before she turned on Max. "Honey isn't a mutt. She's my friend, and more human than a lot of people I know." Her jaundiced look told Max he was included.

Max squared his jaw. Enough was enough. He could be as stubborn as she was. If he didn't get a decent night's rest pretty soon, he wasn't going to be responsible for his actions. "Look, I'm tired and in no mood to put up with any more tonight. Make up your mind, Kelly. It's either the dog or me. You can't have both."

Kelly picked up Honey and gazed around the bedroom. "I guess she can sleep in the chair for tonight. I'll fix it up with pillows."

Max let out his breath. "Thank goodness. For a moment, I thought you were about to choose the mutt."

"It was close," Kelly agreed with a frown. "Very close. I just hope you understand all we're going to do is sleep together. And that's only for appearance' sake."

"You got it," Max answered sourly. He didn't intend to tempt fate any further than he had last night if he could help it. The big problem was the size of the bed they were about to share. If they had been married lovers, instead of married strangers, the size of the bed would have been ideal. ''You act as if last night was all my idea.''

''I'll agree it took the two of us to get into this mess,'' Kelly replied, ''but don't get any wrong ideas. You share the bed, period. You don't share me.''

''Peace!'' Max yawned. ''I'm beat and, come to think of it, I'm starved. I don't remember having anything to eat since coffee and a muffin back at the hotel.''

Kelly took a mental inventory of the kitchen pantry and came up empty. ''Sorry, we don't eat at home very often. Since I work here on the base, it's easier to go over to the officers' mess for dinner.''

Alarmed, Max shook his head. ''No thanks. Not with your father storming around somewhere out there. The last thing I need is to get into a public argument with him on his territory.''

''I'll go take a look in the refrigerator. There's always breakfast cereal,'' Kelly murmured. ''That is, if Sean hasn't emptied the box.'' She led the way to the kitchen and opened a cupboard. ''Sorry, it looks as if the cereal is gone.'' She rummaged in the refrigerator. ''I'm afraid all we have is milk and peanut butter and strawberry jam. Sean lives on peanut butter and jam sandwiches.''

''If they're good enough for a growing boy, they're good enough for me. Look how Sean turned out.'' Max shrugged out of his jacket and hung it on a chair. ''Can I help?''

Kelly blinked when Max rolled up his sleeves and opened his shirt collar. His tanned forearms reminded her of the way his heated skin had slid against hers in the night. Her breasts began to tingle, her skin to warm. She held the cold jar of jam to her warm cheek.

Caught in reliving last night, she didn't realize at first that Max was waiting for an answer. He obviously wanted to help, but the kind of help that preoccupied her at the moment was off-limits. "Sure," she said playfully. "I've always felt marriage should be a partnership." She handed him a loaf of sandwich bread and a jar of chunky peanut butter. "You do the peanut-butter bit and I'll add the jam."

Max unscrewed the jar and took a deep sniff. "This reminds me of the peanut butter cookies our housekeeper makes at home." He ran his finger around the inside edge of the jar, licked his finger and contemplated Kelly. "So, with all this talk about a honeymoon, does it mean you're finally willing to admit we might be married?"

Watching Max lick his finger the way he'd licked her breasts, Kelly almost dropped the jar of jam. Coupled with his agreement they were actually married, she was embarrassed down to her toes. She found herself counting the seeds in the spoonful of strawberry jam she had been about to add to a slice of bread. "Not really married," she corrected. "Only for appearance' sake and only as long as we're on the base, remember? When we're ready to go our separate ways, it'll be a different story."

"Sorry, you can't have it both ways." To Kelly's discomfiture, Max licked the last bit of peanut butter off his fingers. "I figure we might be in this together for a while, so make up your mind. Being on the base has nothing to do with it. Either we're married, or we're not.''

"Together for a while? I thought you agreed this marriage was for only one more day.''

Max winked. "That was then. This is now. Now it's for as long as it takes.''

"Have it your way.'' Kelly ignored his grin and regarded him quizzically. "You act as if you don't mind being married, after all. Isn't there someone back home you care about?''

"A girl back home?'' Max took a bite of his sandwich and munched thoughtfully. "I suppose you could say so if I count Lian Thomas.'' But right now she wasn't back home. She was in Hawaii—waiting for him to join her in a few days.

"Are you going to marry her?'' Kelly's heart skipped a beat. In spite of her original desire to go it alone, she felt a faint regret that Max was taken. Not that she actually cared, she told herself. She was just curious.

"You might say it'll be more of a merger,'' Max answered. "Lian's folks and mine have been business partners for years. The marriage is something our parents have planned for since we were kids.'' He took another large bite of his sandwich and chewed thoughtfully. "Lian's just earned the master's degree in elementary education she's been working for. Last time we spoke, she mentioned getting married this summer.''

"How do *you* feel about that?'' Kelly asked softly. "Or aren't you ready for the marriage?''

Max shrugged. "Like I said, I sort of think of it as

a merger. But one marriage at a time. I have to take care of this one first.''

''A merger? Is that what you think marriages are? What's wrong with falling in love?'' She took two glasses out of a cupboard and handed them to Max.

He poured the milk and reached for another sandwich. ''I guess I haven't given the subject a lot of thought. Marriage isn't on my agenda right now.''

Kelly stopped in midbite. ''On your 'agenda'? A 'merger'? No wonder you're still single. What kind of woman would want you? What kind of a man are you?''

Max took a deep swallow of milk and settled back in a chair. ''In a nutshell, I'm not only methodical, I'm a planner. I've found life to be less complicated that way.''

''But an agenda?'' Kelly's eyes widened. ''How can anyone live by an agenda? What's the fun in that?''

''No problem,'' Max answered. ''Actually, I've had an agenda made for me since I was a kid. Now I make my own. That way I always know exactly what I'm doing and where I'm headed. No impulse, no surprises.'' At the incredulous look on Kelly's face, he frowned. ''You don't agree?''

''No. For all your planning, after last night it looks as if you're just as human as the rest of us. What happened to change your mind?''

You. Max studied his half-empty glass. ''Guess I should have passed on the champagne punch last night and stuck to milk.'' He caught Kelly's doubting gaze and thought back to their conversation in front of the bathroom mirror at the hotel. ''You know, it isn't your forehead that gives you away, Kelly O'Rourke. It's your eyes. Something bothering you?''

"I was just thinking about what you said about planning your life." Kelly fingered her almost untouched sandwich. "I think it's kind of sad. Where's the fun in planning everything? Wouldn't it be more exciting if you left some room for the unexpected?"

"That's precisely the point." Max poured himself another glass of milk. "Interesting, no. Dangerous, yes. I'm not the kind of guy who's comfortable with the unexpected. Look at what happened when I forgot myself last night."

Kelly nibbled at her sandwich. Under the muddied circumstances of their relationship, last night and all that had happened to her was the last thing she wanted to look at comfortably. "That's something else. I believe marriage is for life. When the right man comes along, I'll know. As far as I'm concerned, marriage is one of the most important decisions a person can make. That's why two of my brothers are still single."

"You have a point." Reminded of why he was attracted to Kelly, Max frowned and shoved away the remains of his sandwich. "I guess I never thought of it that way. Until last night, I suppose I just accepted that Lian and I would marry someday."

Her own sandwich forgotten, Kelly stared at Max. No way was he the man for her. Marriage to a pragmatic man like him would leave no room for the magic of falling in love or the exciting challenge of working to keep a marriage together for life. The idea that it had taken champagne punch to humanize him last night was positively mind-boggling.

Adding up the pros and cons of being married to Max, Kelly placed him on her "con" list along with all the traditional and controlling men in her life. The kind of man she was trying to rid herself of. Unfortunately, her "pro" list of men was still blank.

In spite of Max's strong sex appeal and a night spent with him she would remember forever, Kelly tried to make herself believe she was glad he was going to move on. As far as she was concerned, Lian Thomas could have him. "So, what's next on this agenda of yours?"

His answering smile told her he was aware of her opinion of him and his agenda. Not that it mattered. The man was a lady-killer for sure. All the more reason she was determined to put off having to go to bed with him.

She looked out the window where darkness had begun to fall. The lights of the base were coming on Another night faced her, a night that promised to be very different than the last one. Torn with telling the truth and living what she was sure would turn out to be a charade, she was unhappy about being caught in a web of deceit.

She studied the used plates and glasses, the jars of jam and peanut butter. Ordinarily she would have rinsed the dishes and put them in the sink for morning, but not tonight. Tonight she intended to clean the kitchen until it was gleaming and spotless. Anything to put off going to bed with Max.

"Why don't you go into the living room and watch TV? I'll clean up here."

"No way," Max protested. "You said marriage is a partnership, remember?"

"I remember, but this partnership has its limits."
She needed space to cool her thoughts and to find a
way out of the corner she'd painted herself into. "Remember, we're only married while we're on the
base."

"Then, tonight we're married," he said firmly.
"I'll help you clean up and *then* we'll watch TV together before we go to bed." He paused and leered
playfully at Kelly. "Unless you'd rather make it an
early night?"

Kelly smothered a smile as she put the milk into
the refrigerator. She admired Max's style, even if she
wasn't ready to take him on—not again. She'd tried
once before to win the battle of sexual innuendos that
had flared between them, and lost. If she wasn't careful, the chances were she'd lose this time as well.

"You go turn on the television. I'll clean up in
here."

"If you won't change your mind, okay. But I'll
only give you five minutes. If you haven't shown up
by then," he promised, "I'll come get you." On his
way out the door, he turned back. "Oh, by the way,
got any popcorn?"

"I'll look." Popcorn, TV and cuddling on a couch
with a man who was convinced she was his wife! She
gazed wistfully at the kitchen door as it closed behind
Max. The evening was the way she envisioned a real
marriage should be. The thought made her head swim.

"I MADE THE POPCORN." Kelly paused beside the
couch. The TV was on, a commercial blaring a new
Internet service. Max was sound asleep.

His long legs were stretched under the coffee table,

his head rested on a mound of pillows. One hand had fallen across his chest, the other hung loosely by his side. Long golden-brown eyelashes lay on cheeks flushed with sleep. Damn the man, Kelly mused. Even in sleep, he looked sexy and irresistible. She leaned closer. Was he really asleep or was this another act?

"Max, wake up. I made popcorn with melted butter. After I went to the trouble of making it for you, you've got to eat it." She waved the bowl under his nose.

Max continued to breathe heavily. Kelly sighed and sank into the couch to watch TV. She was about to give up when she heard a car drive up outside.

"Max, wake up!" She shook his leg. "Dad's home!"

"That's okay," he murmured. "We're married."

Torn between laughter and frustration, Kelly shook him again. "Wake up. He'll think we're crazy if he comes in and finds you asleep and me watching television."

Groggy, Max slowly came awake. "What's the matter?"

"I said I heard Dad drive into the garage," Kelly answered breathlessly. "Wake up."

Max ran his hand across his forehead. "Sorry, I must have been more beat than I'd realized." He took stock of his surroundings. "What's wrong with my falling asleep on the couch?"

"We're supposed to be newlyweds, that's what's wrong." She held her breath, listened for the sound of a car door closing.

"What's wrong with newlyweds getting some sleep?"

"Max!"

"Okay, okay." He yawned and stretched his arms. "What do you want me to do?"

"I want us to go to bed in my room."

"If going to bed together is what will convince your father we're married, there's no problem," Max answered. He sat up and pulled her down on top of him. Popcorn flew in all directions. The bowl bounced off the wooden floor and rolled into a corner, leaving a trail of buttered popcorn behind it. Honey quivered with delight and licked the floor. "Does this mutt of yours give you any ideas?"

Kelly grabbed him around the neck and hung on for dear life as they rolled off the couch and onto the floor. He found himself nose to nose, lips to lips with an enchanting woman who was growing on him by the minute. Before she could protest, Max stole a kiss.

She tasted of a mixture of peanut butter and jelly, popcorn and salty butter, he thought as he gazed into her eyes. "Too bad your father's home," he murmured into her lips. "I know a great way to eat popcorn."

"Max!" Kelly tried to squirm out of his arms. "Dad will be in here any minute. I don't want him to see us this way."

"I don't see why." He grinned up at her. "If this doesn't convince your father we're married, nothing will."

Kelly gasped, shook popcorn out of her hair and struggled to her feet. "It would only convince him we're both out of our minds. Hurry up, I'll clean up this mess later."

What an odd mixture Kelly was, Max thought as

he helped her up. One moment she was denying they were married, the next, as if the couch-and-popcorn act wasn't convincing enough, she was insisting he sleep with her in her bed. Not that sleeping together was unappealing. He was happy to do his duty. It was trying to honor his promise to keep to himself after she'd declared the bed to be a "hands-off" zone that was the problem.

"Okay," he agreed reluctantly. "But don't blame me if neither of us gets any sleep."

Kelly grabbed his hand and pulled him after her into the bedroom. "Hurry, I just heard Dad close the garage door. You can go into the bathroom to change while I go and say good-night."

"Wait a minute. Where did you say you're going?"

"To say good-night to Dad."

Max held out his hand to stop her. He took a deep breath. "Kelly, I don't know how to say this any more clearly without embarrassing you, but here goes. I'm sure your father doesn't expect a newly married woman to leave her husband's bed and come out to say good-night to her father. Any more than he expects to find me sleeping alone on the couch. You can see him in the morning when you try to explain the popcorn all over the living-room floor."

Kelly blushed. "I guess you're right," she answered. "I'll wait here with Honey while you change."

Moments later, Max came out of the adjoining bathroom dressed in boxer shorts. He shrugged at the look Kelly gave him. "Sorry. I don't have any pajamas. This is the best I can do. I usually sleep in the raw.''

Kelly's hormones raced as she remembered last night, when Max had been nude. And so had she been, except for the garter that had remained on her leg. Tonight, she vowed, was going to be different. No more taking chances, no more encouraging Max. And no more thinking about the night they met.

"If Dad weren't home, I would have borrowed a pair of his pajamas for you without him knowing," she muttered. "But since he's here…"

"I'll go to sleep with what I have," Max finished the sentence for her. He smothered a smile at Kelly's blush. "Let's go to bed."

"In a minute. I have to change." Kelly grabbed her flannel robe from the chair and disappeared into the bathroom.

Max exchanged a long look with Honey, who was looking at him with doggie reproach. "Sorry, you sleep alone. Tonight is my turn." He took the pillows off the bed and put them into the leather chair and added Honey to the nest. Next, he turned down the quilt and surveyed the size of the bed. *Good luck at keeping your distance, Max,* he thought just as Kelly shuffled back into the room.

She wore a pink robe, a matching flannel night-gown buttoned to her neckline and a defiant look. Matching furry slippers were on her feet.

Max thought she was charming. If she thought the old-fashioned granny nightgown was going to keep his thoughts pure and his hands to himself, she was mistaken. He'd seen enough of the real Kelly last night to be able to visualize her rose petal–soft skin and her shapely legs. Memories of sights that made a man's heart beat as if he'd just run a five-mile race. Still, if she wanted to wear the nightgown tonight, it was okay with him. He needed all the help he could get to stay on the straight and narrow.

"Ready for bed?"

"Er...yes, I guess so," Kelly agreed. "You take the inside next to the wall and I'll sleep on the outside."

Max studied the empty bed. "I've been thinking. Unless I'm off on my calculations, I think we can manage only if we sleep like spoons."

"Spoons?" Her eyes seemed to glaze over.

"I'll show you." He got into bed, turned on his right side and held his arms open wide. "Come on, get in."

Kelly stood there staring at the bed.

"Better take off the robe before you get in," Max instructed. "We need every inch of space we can get."

Kelly hesitated, then took off her robe and hurriedly slid under the covers.

"Now, turn on your right side," Max instructed. He pulled her into his arms and covered them with the quilt. "There, that should do it for now," he muttered. "Although I don't know how long this arrangement is going to last."

"Go to sleep," Kelly whispered. "Dad can hear you. His room is on the other side of the wall."

Sleep, she said. Max grimaced. In his arms, Kelly felt warm and soft just the way he remembered. If she only knew the truth. Sometimes the less a man saw of a woman's body, the more erotic the pictures he envisioned.

He lay there, counting sheep, the number of squares on the patchwork quilt and even the number of times he heard Kelly sigh in her sleep. Nothing worked. The night became another test of his manhood.

With his father-in-law on the other side of the wall behind him, and Kelly scrunched into a ball and covered to her chin, as far as Max was concerned, his back was against the wall in more ways than one. If he couldn't resist temptation, he was in deep trouble

Chapter Five

Kelly stared at the dock. "Is *that* Dad's idea of a honeymoon retreat? It looks like something out of a children's book."

Max took a close look. Decorated to resemble a log cabin, the houseboat looked like a giant toy. Sunlight glistened off its red roof. Red-checkered curtains hung at the windows, two wooden deck chairs filled the narrow porch and fishing rods leaned on wooden railings. A couple of float tubes were tied to the handrail. Incongruously, a rambling pink rosebush climbed over a trellis that framed the front door.

Max had to agree the houseboat looked strange. But after an uncomfortable night in the O'Rourke home with doubting eyes on him, he was anxious to find someplace where he and Kelly could have some privacy. "It's a houseboat. Why?"

"Houses belong on dry land. This one floats."

Max smothered a laugh. "That's why it's called a house*boat*."

Kelly didn't look any happier with the explanation than she did when she'd first laid eyes on the boat. "What are we supposed to do with it?"

"I plan on anchoring it in the middle of Lake Mead as soon as we load up with a few things we'll need. Before I'm through," Max assured her, "you'll feel right at home."

Kelly hugged Honey closer. "You're sure you want to go through with this?"

"I'm sure. Besides, we're making your father happy."

Max watched Kelly wilt. "Come on, Kelly, be reasonable," he coaxed. "Since the Sahara was out of the question, this sounds like the next best thing. After the way Patrick kept looking at me, I figure a houseboat is the only sure way to stay out of his sight."

Kelly swallowed hard. While Max had been outside loading their suitcases into the car, she'd overheard Patrick telling her father that Max resembled a con man/gambler in a wanted poster back at the police station. And that he was going to the station to check it out.

Afraid she'd be caught listening, she'd hesitated behind the bedroom door. Clearly it became a case of taking a chance by going along with Max, or remaining at home to try to explain her way out of the mess she was in.

She'd paced the floor, Honey at her heels, while she debated her next move. Set as she was on gaining her freedom, Max had become the obvious choice. After all, she'd reasoned, it wasn't as though the man in the poster was wanted for murder. According to Patrick, the man was a gambler, or even a con man. A con man she could handle.

Besides, Max was Troy's cousin. Surely he or DeeDee would have told her if Max had a record.

"Kelly, is something the matter?"

Kelly closed her eyes. She didn't know which was worse, her upset stomach or the thought of Patrick's suspicions. How could she tell Max what she'd overheard when there was no proof Max was the man the law was looking for? She decided to go with her instincts.

"I still think houses belong on dry land," Kelly answered with a dark look at the bobbing boat. "The last time I was on a boat I got seasick."

"Seasick, on a lake?" Max smothered a desire to laugh. "Come on, Kelly, I'm sure you've lived around here long enough to know there are no swells on Lake Mead. Come on, open your eyes and take a good look. The lake is as smooth as glass. I'm positive there's not enough movement out there to make a ripple."

She opened her eyes and gazed mournfully at the lake. "I'm afraid you're going to have to take my word for it. I feel seasick already."

"Are you sure it's not all in your head?"

Max had barely completed the question when a motorboat raced past, sending the houseboat bobbing up and down in the water, straining at its dock ties.

"I'm sure," Kelly replied balefully. "It's not my head I'm worried about, it's my stomach." To Max's dismay, her complexion turned a pale green as she watched the little house rock and roll.

"If you really want to cancel the honeymoon and go back home..."

From the way Kelly's eyes brightened, Max was

sure she was about to turn on her heel and head for the car. He had to stop her. Going back into the O'Rourke lion's den was the last thing he wanted to do. "Kelly, you don't really want to go home, do you?"

After a quick glance at Max, Kelly turned back to study the houseboat. "No, I guess not," she muttered. "Since Dad went to all this trouble, I suppose it's worth a try. I sure hope it has two beds so we can get a good night's sleep."

"Amen to that," Max said gratefully. He hadn't slept for more than an hour or two last night, and even that had been in short stages. The problem had been less a lack of space than Kelly's tempting proximity. How could a red-blooded man be expected to sleep while holding a delectable woman like Kelly in his arms?

To add to his misery, every time Kelly had turned over in her sleep, he'd been forced to turn over with her or risk having her land on the floor. It seemed to him that he'd spent most of the night with his nose against a blank wall. Or breathing in the tempting scent of aromatic body butter. And all the while mulling over how his comfortable agenda had been shot to hell from the first moment he'd laid eyes on Kelly.

Instead of enjoying a vacation in Vegas and going on to Hawaii, here he was, faced with a reluctant bride and an unexpected honeymoon.

In retrospect, maybe he should have confessed to her father that he wasn't sure he and Kelly were actually married. Taken his chances and bowed out of the picture—until and unless honor called him to face any consequences. But after one long look at Kelly's face when confronted by her father, he'd known where his duty lay. What was another day or two until he could get away on the vacation he felt he so richly deserved?

His final decision to go through with a honeymoon had been cemented when Patrick had shown up this morning and asked to see a marriage certificate and Max's social security number. He'd pretended to be outraged, more to stall for time than to fight for his honor. How could he admit he didn't have a clue about the certificate? As for his social security number, hell would have had to freeze over before he would have obliged. As far as he'd known, he hadn't broken any law when he'd married Kelly.

He would have felt a lot better about the state of affairs if he hadn't seen Patrick eyeing him suspiciously before they'd left this morning.

He glanced at the receipt for the houseboat rental marked "Paid by credit card." Eighty-five dollars a day to keep him and Kelly close must have been worth every penny to Michael O'Rourke.

If the man only knew that once they were anchored out on the water, Max was sure it was just going to be a matter of time before he could head back to Las Vegas under the cover of night.

In the meantime, the houseboat was a perfect hideaway until he could think of a way for Kelly and himself to fade out of sight. So far, so good.

On the other hand, he thought as he warily contemplated Kelly's wan complexion, maybe he was congratulating himself too soon.

Now to convince Kelly they were doing the sensible thing by accepting her father's wedding present.

"Want to go on board and look around? If you're still unhappy after that, we'll forget it."

Kelly came to with a start. Now that she'd actually talked herself into a queasy stomach, she had no choice but to give the boat a try. Thankfully, the lake was quiet again.

"The only thing missing is Granny Clampett," she announced, her voice dark with misery. "Are you sure this tug has hot-and-cold running water?"

"Yes, I'm sure." Max studied the rental brochure. "Just try to remember the point of this honeymoon is to satisfy your father and to keep out of your brothers' sight."

Kelly's heart did a flip-flop. Maybe getting out of her brothers' sight wasn't a good idea after all. What if Max *was* a con man? Maybe her father had been right: she was too impulsive for her own good.

Of course, there was Honey, a good watchdog when it came to Max. Already suspicious of Max's intentions, Honey seemed committed to keeping him in line.

"I'm still not sure this is a good idea," Kelly announced glumly. "If the honeymoon was intended to help us get out of town without anyone noticing us, we're in trouble. How are we going to get away if we're stuck in the middle of Lake Mead?"

Max explained about the dinghy tied to the back of the houseboat. "I've already checked everything out. Just try to remember that unless you want to hang around the base being grilled by this Father Joe, we have to stall for time. Right about now, I doubt I could cross the state line with you without Patrick hearing about it."

Cold shivers played a chorus across Kelly's spine. She met Max's gaze and thought hard about having placed herself in the middle of a lake with a man she hardly knew. His expression was friendly enough, his lips curved in a reassuring smile. His thoughts, reflected in his soft brown eyes, appeared harmless.

Her instincts told her Max was an honest and decent man, if slightly misguided. How many men could dream up a wedding and insist it had been real? "I suppose you're right," she finally agreed and reluctantly studied her surroundings. "The outside of that thing you call a house looks like something out of a TV movie. I hope the inside is more modern than it looks from here."

"It is," Max assured her. "At least it is in the brochure. We'll have to round up a couple of sleeping bags, fill the gas tank and get enough food for a day or two," Max went on, checking the list that came with the brochure. "I noticed a shop here onshore that should have what we need. Maybe we can have some fun with this honeymoon after all."

Another speedboat raced by. "I wouldn't bet on it," Kelly muttered, rubbing her stomach.

"Do you want to come shopping with me, or do you want to wait here?"

"I suppose I might as well try the boat," Kelly answered reluctantly. "Besides, I don't trust Honey in a market. Just don't forget to add dog food to the list."

Max traded thoughtful glances with Kelly's pet. He hadn't been prepared to believe a dog could understand human speech or read human minds, but from the way the mutt kept watching him, he was rapidly becoming a believer. "Think you can keep the two of you from falling overboard?"

"No problem," Kelly answered resolutely. "Just don't be long. Honey missed breakfast."

"So did I," Max muttered to Kelly's retreating back. With no officer's mess in sight, and very little besides last night's dinner of peanut butter and jam sandwiches under his belt, he was beginning to wonder if the reason the O'Rourkes ate at the officers' mess was that Kelly didn't know how to cook.

WITH MAX OUT OF SIGHT, Kelly clutched Honey to her hip and gingerly made her way across the narrow gangplank onto the deck of the houseboat.

The living area looked decent enough, she decided gratefully. She surveyed a corner couch, a narrow table and a television set mounted on the wall. A steering wheel and a panel of gadgets she assumed Max would need to steer the boat filled the wall under the front window.

A small, compact kitchen with a microwave oven and barbecue and a small refrigerator completed the room.

Her gaze swung back to the steering wheel. Did Max even know how to drive a houseboat? The thought that he might be a novice at boating sent shivers up and down her spine and set the butterflies in her stomach fluttering. Her always overactive imagination saw them drifting right over the top of Hoover Dam.

Swallowing the lump in her throat, she clutched Honey and moved on through a narrow hallway to the bedroom.

The size of the stripped-down bed was an improvement over her own narrow bed at home. Not exactly a double, it was larger than a twin. Not that it made a difference. The way she felt right now, another human body holding her would be a comfort. Even if it belonged to Max.

Sleeping like spoons with him last night hadn't been as bad as she'd expected, either, she mused as she mentally measured the bed in front of her. She hadn't told him, but she'd actually enjoyed his firm masculine strength, the warmth of his body wrapped around hers, his breath on the back of her neck. The only real problem had been that every time she'd wiggled to make herself comfortable, Max had sighed in her ear. And whenever she'd turned over, she'd found them nose to nose.

She hadn't exactly minded that, either. At least they could have talked or shared a kiss or two if Max had been willing to cooperate. Instead, he'd muttered under his breath and turned over to face the wall.

Of course, her attraction for Max predated the conversation between Patrick and her father she'd overheard this morning. Still, forewarned was forearmed. From now on, she intended to keep her emotions out of their relationship until she could make a graceful exit.

Maybe Max's attitude about agendas was just as well, Kelly decided. No impulse, no surprises, Max had told her, and he was probably right. Especially since they didn't really know each other very well and intended to say goodbye soon.

"THERE!" Max carefully steered the boat out of its slip and made for open water. He gestured to the bags of groceries he'd purchased ashore. "How about if I start up the barbecue as soon as I anchor, and you put on the steaks I bought for dinner?"

"Sorry," Kelly answered. Her stomach rebelled at the thought of steaks. "I don't think I can handle steaks right this minute." She turned her head away from the bloodred meat Max had laid out on the small stainless-steel counter. "The truth is, if it doesn't come out of a can I don't know what to do with it."

She was struck by a more important question. Dinner, whichever form it would eventually take, could wait. "By the way, you *do* know how to handle a boat?"

"Sure," Max answered. "We have a family yacht anchored on the Charles River. Piece of cake."

They were interrupted by a frantic yelp and the sound of a loud splash. Kelly turned pale and started for the door. "Honey!"

"I told you to keep an eye on the mutt," Max bellowed. He stopped the engine, secured the steering wheel and beat Kelly to the door. Sure enough, there was Kelly's mutt paddling for dear life. "Wait here," he shouted and began to pull off his shoes.

Shrieking to Honey to hang on, Kelly grabbed a life preserver and threw it. Instead of going overboard, the hard life preserver hit Max square in the head as he was about to dive into the lake.

Max flailed as he fell into the water, and took in a mouthful of water. He could hear Honey furiously paddling beside him. He didn't know if the mutt could swim or not—he had to save her. What a helluva way to start a honeymoon, real or not.

Gasping for air, he grabbed the dog by the collar and held her out of the water while he kicked to the boat. He could hear Kelly hollering and offering to help, but he didn't have time or breath to reply. Besides, he didn't need any more of her kind of help.

"Good shot," he gasped when he finally reached the side of the boat. He hung on to the anchor rope while he caught his breath. "Untie the rope ladder and throw it over the side!"

Unfortunately, Kelly took him literally and threw the ladder over the side. This time, thank God, she narrowly missed him. "Hold out your hands!" he shouted. When Kelly hung over the side of the boat, he handed Honey up to her. Muttering curses under his breath, he retrieved the ladder and climbed onto the boat, staggering onto the deck and falling to his knees. He spat out a mouthful of water. "What were you trying to do, drown me?"

"I'm sorry. I was just trying to help." She put Honey on the deck, knelt beside Max and began to pound him on the back. In between blows, she tried to wipe the water out of his eyes. "Are you sure you're okay now?"

"Hey, lay off, will you," Max hollered, fending off Kelly with one arm and her mutt with another. "Give me a chance to catch my breath."

With Honey shaking herself to rid herself of water and licking his face in gratitude, Max felt overwhelmed by the unwanted attention. His heart was still racing and the granddaddy of all headaches was about to send him over the edge. At the moment, he wasn't all that sure the attention was worth drowning for. Sure, he was touched by her concern, but she and her mutt had been the cause of the problem to begin with. He struggled to untangle himself and regain his feet.

"Here, let me help you." Kelly grabbed him by the arm and pulled. Before Max could protest, she slipped on the wet deck and tumbled on top of him.

Max lay back on the deck, staring at a darkening sky and drearily cursing his fate. No matter his good intentions—popcorn episode excluded—he and Kelly kept falling over each other. Still, he thought wearily, he'd never been one to pass up an opportunity when it presented itself. He met her eyes and tried to grin. "A great beginning for a honeymoon," he said. "This ought to convince anyone watching from shore that we're married."

"Watching? From where? I don't see anything...." Kelly gazed nervously around her. "Are you sure?"

"There's one thing more to make it look good. We need to kiss."

"To kiss?" Kelly stared down at him. The blow on his head was worse than she'd thought. "Here? Now? Why?"

"Sure," Max answered seriously. "We have to appear to be loving newlyweds, don't we?"

Kelly stared into his golden-brown eyes. Sure enough, a faint sign of laughter glinted there. And some other emotion that sent an answering response through her. How could she be so sexually aware of the man when all she was trying to do was save his life?

"Don't be ridiculous," she managed to say. "Except for a speedboat or two, we're practically alone on the lake. There isn't anyone watching, and you know it. What are you up to?''

"Collecting my reward for saving the mutt,'' Max moved under her. ''So, how about the kiss?''

It took Kelly a few seconds to realize the position she was in wasn't helping to lighten up the situation. How could she be serious when she was lying on top of an all-male, testosterone-laden man like Max? ''Sorry,'' she said as she scrambled to her feet. ''I didn't mean to hurt you. I was just trying to help.''

''Anytime,'' Max said with a fatalistic shrug. ''Although, for a while I thought the mutt was more important to you than I was.'' His grin faded when he looked up and saw the look in Kelly's eyes.

He saw an echo of his own growing awareness of their mutual attraction. An attraction heightened by the intimate contact of nights together. And now feminine curves outlined by sodden clothing.

What had started out to be a joke suddenly turned real. He *wanted* to kiss Kelly, to have her kiss him back. He *wanted* to take her in his arms and create new memories to add to the old.

The realization that he was attracted to Kelly in ways he hadn't imagined possible caught him by surprise. They were each too different, too strong-willed to make a go of any kind of a relationship. Kelly wanted her freedom. There was still his agenda to think of.

Impossible! Yet, gazing into Kelly's eyes, he was tempted to try.

With Kelly still in his arms, Max managed a good look at Honey, who lay watching him, panting and moaning in a way it seemed only dogs could. She behaved as if she knew he'd saved her life, her usual dark look had turned to one of adoration. Not even Kelly got in the way.

Max smothered a groan. Sure as hell, the mutt had adopted him.

"Are you sure you're okay?" Kelly asked anxiously. "You really ought to change before you catch cold. You're soaking wet."

Max wiped away the water that dripped from his hair and down his neck. He regarded the motorboat that was sweeping by them at sixty miles an hour. "I guess I do look kind of stupid."

Kelly shook her head. To a casual bystander, Max might look like a man who'd lost his mind and gone swimming in his clothes. But she knew the truth; he was a romantic hero.

The way his wet clothing clung to him sent her thoughts and hormones into a tailspin. She remembered seeing him partially undressed the night he'd claimed was their wedding night. Now, with his dripping jeans, his narrow hips and muscular thighs left little to the imagination.

"As a matter of fact," Max said, "you look a little damp yourself. Mighty interesting, too."

Kelly sat up and glanced down at the drenched sweater that outlined her breasts and their taut nipples. She hurriedly crossed her arms across her chest and rose to her feet. "Excuse me while I go in and change." She squared her jaw and turned her back. "Come on," she told a reluctant Honey. "I'll get you dried off, too."

"Kelly?"

She turned back at Max's call. She was already

burning up. One more suggestive remark and she was going to push him back into the lake. "What now?"

He grinned and bounded to his feet. "I don't think you're seasick anymore."

"You're right." She burst into laughter. How could she keep from laughing at this entire scenario? Poor Honey, too, was still shaking water out of her fur.

"I have something to tell you. Just give me a few minutes to catch my breath." He carefully skirted the damp and shivering canine cause of their problem. He threw a wet arm around Kelly's shoulders and walked with her into the cabin. "You want to change first?"

Before what? Kelly wondered. She ducked her head so Max couldn't see the flush that came over her face. "Sure. I'll be right back." She rushed across the cabin, grabbed a towel from the pile of linens on the bed and threw it to Max. "Here. You can change out there."

In the safety of the small bedroom, Kelly hurried to dry herself off then took a stab at drying a struggling Honey. "Are you decent?" she called to Max after she'd changed into fresh jeans and a voluminous flannel shirt.

"You might say that," he answered. "Come ahead."

Kelly came into the tiny living room to find Max wearing jeans, a floral Hawaiian shirt and sandals on his feet. She took a second look. "Exactly what are you dressed for?"

"Hawaii," he answered succinctly. "I was going there for a vacation when this wedding of ours interrupted me."

Now that Kelly felt safe enough with Max to joke

around with him, she grinned. "Sorry about that. Maybe you can take it later."

"I don't think so." Now that his agenda was shot to hell, Max wasn't sure he wanted to go to Hawaii anyway. Not as long as he was enjoying his unexpected honeymoon with Kelly.

He rummaged in the bags of groceries with Honey sniffing at his heels. "Wine? It'll warm you up."

"No thanks," Kelly answered, trying to ignore Max's sheer masculinity. His tight jeans and the Hawaiian shirt he was wearing were positively disconcerting. "I'm warm enough already. What did you want to ask me?"

Max opened the bottle of wine and poured himself a drink. "Only that I was wondering why an attractive woman like you doesn't feel she's ready to be married."

"Is that all?" She wandered over to the couch and sat down. "The truth is, I just don't want to have to answer to anyone. Not now, and maybe not later, either."

"Not ever?"

"Not until I've had a chance to try life on my own," Kelly answered firmly. "I want to be able to make my own decisions, do some of the things I've dreamed about all my life. I've never had a chance with Dad on my heels and moving us every few years."

"It's a big world out there," Max tasted the wine, nodded approval and sipped some more. "Are you sure you're ready for it?"

"I've seen more of the world than most people my age, but I'll never know for sure until I've tried." She smiled bashfully. "Actually, everything was fine until I turned thirteen. That was when my family started treating me as if I'd break."

She looked up to see Max regarding her with a half smile on his lips. "You've never looked fragile to me," he said, rubbing the back of his head. "In fact, you've got a mean throwing arm."

"That's the point, I'm *not* fragile," she agreed. "With three brothers to compete against, I was a tomboy. Most of the kids I hung around with were boys. That is, until…" She hesitated. "Anyway, Mom decided it was time for me to act like a girl. I didn't like the idea, but moving the way we did, I never had a chance to really assert myself."

"That doesn't sound like the Kelly I know." Max laughed. "I feel as if we've been in a sparring match from the moment we met."

"That's because you dared me." Kelly's pragmatic glance challenged him to try. "No one dares an Irish person and gets away with it."

Max held up his hands. "No contest, although I seem to remember we both won *that* dare."

Kelly felt herself blush as she recalled their "wedding night."

"When Mom died, Dad, Damon and Patrick continued to treat me as if I were a valuable piece of glass. Remaining a tomboy was out." She frowned at the memory. "Sometimes I feel as if I've been programmed to be a little Goody Two-shoes. The fact is, no matter how hard I try, actually I'm not." She gazed meaningfully at Max and was pleased to see him flush.

"Anyway, now that DeeDee's married and moving

away from Las Vegas, I've decided to go out on my own too. Just the way you men do. So don't take it personally,'' she added with a grin, ''but the last thing I need right now is another man in my life.''

''Well,'' Max said, ''it sounds to me as if your father knows you better than you think he does. You *are* a rebel.''

When Kelly said she'd felt as though she'd been programmed, it occurred to him she could have been talking about himself. If Kelly thought her father was controlling, she should have known his own parents. The only problem he could see was that Kelly didn't value herself enough.

He thought back to the time he'd gone off to boarding school as a small, carefree kid. From that time on, the hours, the days and the weeks of his life had been planned for him. Even now, the old habits of planning future agendas persisted.

It wouldn't have been so bad if he'd been able to choose the major milestones of his life himself. He hadn't; not the succession of private boarding schools, the university he'd attended or the career in his father's business. Even the vacation he'd intended to take had been orchestrated for him by Lian, a woman to whom he was nominally engaged.

He thought about the difference between Lian and Kelly. Lian was as predictable as her agendas. Kelly was his chance to do the first truly impulsive thing in his entire life. In his present mood, Kelly won hands down.

As for Lian, if he didn't join her in a couple of days, he'd have to think of something to tell her. But now there was Kelly to enjoy.

He made a mental note to add Lian to the list of telephone calls he had to make as soon as he was alone.

Meeting Kelly's candid gaze, her way of thinking began to seem a hell of a lot more attractive than Lian's or his own. After he untangled the nonsense that had brought him and Kelly together, he was going to take a long look at his life. Maybe it was time for him to rethink his agenda. He'd been deaf, dumb and blind to the truth long enough.

"Well, Kelly O'Rourke," Max finally answered. "I guess you've got something there. I wish you luck. But I'm not sorry about the wonderful night we spent together."

Kelly's complexion paled. He took her hands in his. "Maybe it won't be as bad as you think. What do you say, shall we try to make a go of it for now?"

"I guess so," she replied. "But remember, without a marriage certificate to prove we were married, this is just a charade. We'll go our own ways later. Right?"

Max nodded reluctantly. Surprisingly enough, considering the circumstances, he wasn't looking forward to the day when they would split, after all. He was beginning to actually like and respect Kelly. More than that, he suddenly found himself anxious to be her husband.

Finding the all-important marriage certificate suddenly became the most important item in his life. "Right," he answered. "This is all a charade...for now."

Chapter Six

Kelly's tailored black woolen slacks fit her like a glove. Her loose dark green shirt turned her Irish eyes into a multicolored kaleidoscope. To add to her charm, her freshly shampooed hair shone like burnished copper.

As far as Max was concerned, the honeymoon could have begun that night.

Even Honey was cooperating. Freshly bathed, the dog drowsed on the window seat with one eye open.

The small table was set with a red cloth and colorful pottery dishes. The wine bottle and a single glass waited.

"Looking good." He sauntered into the small dining area. "I'm as hungry as a bear."

"We are, too."

"We?"

"Honey and me."

Max sighed and exchanged a piercing look with Honey, the bodyguard. Now that he and Kelly had reached an amicable truce, he would have preferred to be alone with her.

Kelly smiled apologetically. "I opened a can of

dog food for Honey. I made a salad and warmed up the frozen stuffed potatoes for us. I'm afraid that's as far as I got.''

"No problem," Max answered with a wry smile. "Actually, I was afraid it was going to have to be peanut butter and jam sandwiches again.''

Kelly laughed. "Is your stomach all you can think about?''

"Not all the time." Max moved to Kelly's side, lifted a cluster of copper hair off her shoulders and let it slide slowly through his fingers. "Actually, I'd begun to remember a great deal more than peanut butter and jam sandwiches.''

Kelly warmed at the sensuous tone in Max's voice. Now that he was starting to remember details about the night they met, the sexual electricity between them was stronger than ever. "If you're referring to what happened the other night, it's never going to happen again." At his understanding grin, Kelly protested. "I mean it. It was a foolish mistake.''

"Never is a long time," he answered with a smile that took aim at her heart and found its target. "Those expressive eyes of yours are telling me a different story.''

He was standing so close, she could feel his body heat. Mesmerized, she blushed.

"Your mind may be saying no, Kelly," he went on, "but your eyes are saying yes." He bent to meet her lips and kissed her denials away.

Mistake or not, she thought as his kisses deepened, the attraction that had drawn her to him at DeeDee's wedding was there, stronger than ever. He could be so strong, yet so tender. And not ashamed to show it.

She'd never met a man like him before, nor had she expected to.

"This has to be wrong," she whispered into his lips. "We hardly know each other."

Max smothered the obvious retort. "We know each other better than you think, or this attraction wouldn't be enough to bring us together," he murmured into the nape of her neck. He chuckled when she shivered under his lips, shifted his attention and gently kissed the corners of her eyes, the tip of her nose. "Right?"

"Maybe so, but this can't be enough." Kelly willed herself to remember it was no use getting in any deeper. Not when they'd both agreed they were to go their separate ways. "I've always wanted to believe there should be more than a physical attraction to bring two people together." She looked up into his eyes. "I want to be loved for myself."

"There is that," Max agreed playfully. "But let me count the ways I'm attracted to you." He held up five fingers. "I like your quick mind." He folded down one finger. "I like the way you take a dare." He folded down another. "I like the way you stand up for yourself when you think you're right." Another finger folded. "I even like your sense of humor." He went on to outline her lips with a tender forefinger.

"That only makes four." Fascinated by the sound of his melodic voice and the tender look in his eyes, Kelly hesitated. Any more of this method of convincing her and she'd be in danger of forgetting why she and Max didn't suit. "You've forgotten number five."

"That's easy." He ran his finger over her cheek.

"I like your combination of sugar and spice. Of never knowing what's going to happen next whenever we're together. I've never felt this way before, and I confess I like it." He glanced over at the window seat. "Given time, I might even get to like the mutt, er…Honey."

Honey perked up when she heard her name. She sat up, wagged her tail and made puppy noises.

Kelly held Max's hand in hers. "Okay. I give in. You almost have me convinced."

"Almost?"

"Yes," she answered shyly. She would have had to be made of stone to resist that sensuous invitation in his voice.

"Well, that's a start, anyway. But let's not forget the physical attraction. The man-woman thing, okay?"

"I'll try." She rested her cheek against Max's chest and listened to the rapid beat of his heart. Forget the man-woman thing? How could she when every beat of his heart echoed hers.

Throwing good intentions aside, Kelly gave in to impulse and unbuttoned his floral shirt. With his twinkling eyes daring her, she ran her hands over his warm, bare chest. "I'm almost there," she said.

He captured her lips in his and kissed her into silence. "Almost isn't enough. Here, let me try again." He kissed the sensitive spot between her breasts.

Kelly was lost. In spite of her traditional upbringing, she'd never willingly stood by passively and let life pass her by. She'd done her best to be the woman her father wanted her to be, not always with success, as her father had reminded her. But she'd always believed the right moment and the right man would come along to free her to be the woman she dreamed of being. DeeDee and Troy's wedding had been the right moment. Was Max the right man?

"What happened to that safe and sane agenda you keep talking about?" she went on to remind them both. "And there's Lian, the girl you said is waiting for you back East."

"She's in Hawaii," he answered absently, "but that was in another lifetime. This is now. I'm going to call her tomorrow and tell her I'm delayed by important business. Besides—" he kissed her lightly and stared deep into her eyes "—I don't need anyone else but you. You are my wife."

"Only when we're on the base. Otherwise, not unless and until you can prove we're married."

Honey began to whimper. Kelly pulled away reluctantly. "She's hungry. I have to feed her."

Max started for the ship's phone. She wanted proof? He'd get it. "While you're at it, I'll make a few telephone calls. I'll see if I can talk to Reggie Bennett about the missing marriage certificate. And, if I have to, I'll call the all-night marriage-license bureau at the Las Vegas City Hall. If we took out a marriage license, they'll know." He picked up the phone, jiggled the instrument panel. To his chagrin, the phone line was dead. Short of going back to the marina, the phone calls would have to wait until morning. Tomorrow was Monday. First thing in the morning they'd head into Vegas and go to the marriage-license bureau—and the city hall, if they had to.

"What's the matter?" Kelly asked.

Max told her about the phone—or lack thereof.

"How about a cell phone? Surely a man like you must have one."

He decided to ignore the comment and not press her on what exactly she meant. "It may come as a surprise to you, but I intended to stay out of reach for a while. I'm supposed to be on vacation."

Kelly sighed. "I know—and I'm grateful." She left to feed Honey.

Mentally cursing at the fates that seemed to be conspiring against him, Max paced the small cabin floor. Every time he tried to add up the pieces, something or someone stopped him. Were the fates trying to tell him he belonged with Kelly?

Not that he needed a wedding certificate to convince him he and Kelly were husband and wife. He was beginning to *feel* married, not that he was sure why. Maybe because he was surrounded by all the trappings of a marriage.

All through dinner, he couldn't stop the picture of a family from painting his mind. He was in the company of an intelligent and sexy woman—even if she had a quirk or two. And there might be a baby. Hell, he'd even acquired a pet dog.

It was Kelly he had to convince that everything was falling into place. She might keep insisting she wasn't ready to be married, but that wasn't his only concern. The real issue, now that her father had brought up the subject, was if she was ready for the possibility she might become a mother.

Max was a man who didn't take his responsibilities lightly, fatherhood included. He'd stick by Kelly.

He heard Kelly in the bedroom, preparing for bed. When the sliver of light under the door disappeared, he thought of joining her. He cursed the fates that prevented him from getting his hands on proof of their married state, from sharing Kelly's bed tonight.

He poured himself the remains of the bottle of wine they'd shared for dinner and dourly surveyed the couch where he'd be spending the night. He only had himself to blame. Right in the middle of a kiss that had set off Fourth of July fireworks he'd managed to say the one thing sure to set Kelly off. "Wife." The result: she was sleeping alone in the small bedroom. He was sleeping with the mutt.

He tried to mold his body into position on the curved couch and cursed when his bare feet encountered Honey's cold, wet nose. Much to his dismay, the mutt had changed its allegiance from Kelly and was sticking to him like glue.

The least he'd envisioned when he'd flown west to Las Vegas to his cousin's wedding Friday night had been a weekend fling at the gaming tables and then on to a week under the Hawaiian skies. Instead, here he was stuck in the middle of Lake Mead straddling the Nevada-Arizona borders. Instead of sleeping with the woman he was sure was his wife, he had a dog as his companion.

It was more than any man should be expected to bear.

SOMEONE WAS KISSING his toes!

For a moment, Max perked up. No, he realized with a deep sigh, someone was *licking* his toes.

He would have given anything to have the someone be Kelly. But after the polite but cool way they'd parted company last night, he wasn't prepared to bet on it. The way his luck was going, the someone was that mutt of hers.

"Cut it out," he growled and covered his legs with the sleeping bag. "Go find Kelly."

"She's already found me," Kelly's voice sounded behind him. "We've been up for ages. She's trying to tell you she's hungry."

Max struggled to sit up. The houseboat was rocking so violently, he fell back against the pillows he'd hijacked from the bedroom last night. "What's wrong with the boat?"

"A high wind came up early this morning while you were sleeping," Kelly answered as she balanced her way across the small kitchen floor. She grabbed a box of cereal that teetered on the edge of the sink. "It always does in winter. Ready for breakfast?"

Max tried to think. The thought of food made his stomach wince, his head ache. He couldn't have eaten a single bran flake if his life had depended on it. Was seasickness catching?

"No thanks," he answered. "You go ahead, don't wait for me. And feed the mutt while you're at it. She's already started on my toes." He gathered the little strength he had and attempted to cover his feet with the sleeping bag he'd used as a blanket.

"Sorry, I've tried," Kelly answered with undisguised good humor. "It looks to me as if she's set her heart on you."

Max's head was throbbing. The movement of the boat wasn't helping and being eaten alive didn't sound very appealing. "Not for breakfast, I hope."

"No. She wants you to feed her." Kelly tried to smother her laughter, but she was too late.

Max had the sinking feeling Kelly was right. He'd never owned a dog, didn't know what to do with a dog and didn't care to learn. "Why me?"

"Some animals will only take food from the person they've bonded with," Kelly explained. "Since she's obviously decided you saved her life, I guess you're the one."

"Lucky me." His dejected gaze strayed from the dog to its sexy owner. For a woman who'd claimed just looking at water made her ill, Kelly looked damn perky this morning. Even her bright green eyes sparkled with good health. Whatever miracle had cured her, he prayed some of it would rub off on him.

He stared down at the mutt, his new dependent. Now that she had his attention, her tail was wagging expectantly.

"I have a suggestion," Max said politely. "Why don't you let her watch you eat breakfast. Maybe she'll get the idea."

"I've already had cereal and bananas." Kelly smiled cheerfully. "Are you sure you're not hungry?"

"No thanks." Max gave up. Either Kelly had the heart of a Good Samaritan or she enjoyed seeing him suffer. "No wonder the mutt's so persistent," he said darkly. "She learned the art from you. If you have any compassion in your heart, please take your mutt out of my sight and feed her."

"You have to stop calling Honey a mutt." Kelly frowned a warning even as she smiled at her pet. "You're going to hurt her feelings."

"I wish. Then maybe she'll leave me alone." Max

muttered a curse when the nylon sleeping bag slipped off the couch.

Honey resumed her assault on his feet.

Max winced. "Doesn't she realize I'm probably just passing through? What's she going to do when I'm gone?"

To Max's surprise, Kelly seemed to sober at the questions. Maybe he was growing on her, he thought with satisfaction. Maybe she'd be willing to come up with an idea to help him in his search for the certificate instead of insisting he do it himself. Marriage to him couldn't be all that bad.

"I'll try to explain annulment or divorce to her when the time comes," Kelly replied. "In the meantime, she's yours."

Max's stomach roiled with the rocking movement of the boat. "Too bad," he said faintly. "If I'm going to die, I'd rather do it privately."

Kelly's expression turned to concern. "You really don't feel well, do you?"

Bleary-eyed, Max watched Kelly balance her way across the small room. He consoled himself with the knowledge there was a tender look in her eyes.

"I hate to tell you this, but you look terrible." To his surprise, she bent over and kissed him on the forehead. She felt his forehead. "I don't have a thermometer handy, but your forehead does feel a little warm. Maybe you *are* coming down with something."

Kelly's kiss diverted Max's attention from his stomach. He was about to ask her not to stop with his forehead, but even in his misery he sensed it was no time for comedy. Not when Kelly took her doctoring seriously. "Do you always kiss a person's forehead when he's sick?"

"Only when there's no thermometer handy." She patted him on the shoulder. "It's an old-country method my mother taught me of testing for fever. But don't worry. I don't think your fever is high enough to be concerned."

"Oh." Max thought of insisting he was burning up with fever so she would test-kiss him some more. On the other hand, maybe she had some kind of tender loving care for a stomachache. "Maybe it was something I ate last night." After assuring Kelly that seasickness was a state of mind, how could he confess he was seasick without embarrassing himself?

To add to his misery, the boat continued to rock. "How come you didn't tell me about the high winds around here before I agreed to let your father rent this thing?"

"You didn't ask," Kelly rescued the sleeping bag from the floor, covered his feet and tucked him in. "Living with an all-male family, I've given up trying to make a man see reason. None of you seems to be able to take it. It's easier to let you find out for yourselves."

Max groaned as another gust of wind came up and the boat strained against its anchor. "So you're willing to let me die?"

"You're not going to die," Kelly assured him. "And furthermore, I don't think there was anything wrong with dinner last night. What you have is a simple case of seasickness."

"There's nothing simple about seasickness," Max said with all the dignity he could muster. He covered his mouth with one hand. His other hand was busy trying to keep Honey from sliding across the room. He was in no condition to rescue the mutt again. "For your information, I feel as if I'm going to—" He jumped up, ran out on deck and hung over the railing.

Kelly came up behind him and patted him on the back. "The fresh air will do you good."

Max scowled into the swells that rocked the boat. "Not if I die first."

"Maybe we ought to go home," Kelly offered when Max finally sagged against the railing. She glanced heavenward. "From the color of the sky, I think a storm is definitely on the way. Take a look."

He smothered a groan. "I'll take your word for it. The only thing I want to look at at the moment is dry land."

"I know just how you feel," Kelly soothed. She led him back into the cabin where she'd tied Honey into a chair with the tablecloth. "Now that the winds are picking up, I definitely think we ought to head for home." Max groaned his agreement. "I'll pull up anchor while you get the boat started."

For a moment, Max felt too sick to think of going back to Las Vegas or riding out the storm. The accelerated rocking movement of the houseboat made up his mind for him. "Sure. Just give me a minute or two to get my act together." He studied Kelly intently. "How come you're not seasick anymore?"

"I decided you were right, that it was all in my mind," she answered cheerfully. "So, how about it? Breakfast or home?"

Max traded a baleful look with the mutt who by now was loose and sitting on his stomach. "Home."

"WANT ME TO DRIVE?"

"Please do," Max answered politely. He gathered their belongings and threw them in the trunk of the car. "I'll just sit here quietly and enjoy the desert scenery."

Kelly smothered a facetious reply. Max's lips were white, his eyes bleary and red and his complexion deathly pale. He looked sick, but she had to admire his fortitude.

She thought back to the way he'd stood up to her father and faced down her brother Patrick for her sake. He'd not only been heroic, he'd been a lot more decisive than he looked right now. After saving her pet, he deserved more than humorous remarks.

She handed him a peppermint candy from a trove she had in her purse. "Here, maybe this will help settle your stomach."

"I wouldn't bet on it," he answered with a soft groan, "but thanks."

On the ride back to Las Vegas, Kelly kept glancing at Max to see if he was okay. He was still green around the eyes, but luckily he'd fallen asleep. Honey, fed her breakfast by a seasick Max, was buckled into a seat belt on the back seat. Even the dog seemed to appreciate the need for quiet sympathy.

By the time they reached the outskirts of Boulder City, Max's breathing was beginning to return to normal. The storm that had driven them off the Colorado River was threatening overhead.

"Where to?" Kelly asked. "A hotel or home?"

Max stirred. "Home. I promised your father we'd come back as soon as the honeymoon was over."

"It's definitely over," Kelly replied, lulling her

clamoring hormones to sleep. To her surprise, she actually felt sorry that their honeymoon had ended so abruptly. Or that their honeymoon had ended before they'd had a chance to sleep together on the boat. Would Max still try to leave once he'd fulfilled the promise he'd made to her father?

She eyed Max's grim visage, then looked away. How could she add to the problem by telling him about her brother's suspicions?

Although her brother's conversation had left her with a vague uneasiness, she felt she knew enough about Max's personality by now to know he wasn't a gambler. If marriage hadn't been on his agenda, she thought with a repressed giggle, gambling certainly wasn't. After all, wasn't marriage a gamble, too?

As for his being a con man... That was another matter, she mused as large raindrops hit the windshield. He was. Hadn't he somehow mesmerized her into going to bed with him when all she'd intended was to put him on? And wasn't he insisting they were married when she was just as sure they were not? But what was there to con her out of, anyway?

She glanced over at Max's chiseled profile. He was too sexy, too attractive for her own good. Being alone with him tonight wasn't such a good idea. Hadn't she seen the flash of desire cross his eyes when she'd tested his forehead for fever? With Max, maybe her single bed back at the base wasn't a good idea.

"Are you sure you want to go back to my place?"

"Yes." Max straightened in his seat. "A promise is a promise. I never break my word if I can help it." His expression became grim. "Even if it means I'm asking for trouble."

"What kind of trouble?" Kelly waited for the answer with bated breath. If Max was ever going to confess he was wanted by the law, now was the time.

"Who knows?" Max shrugged. "I noticed the look in your brother's lawman eyes. And after I turned down his request for my social security number, I could see he had something on his mind. In fact, I wouldn't be surprised to find him waiting for us."

"Maybe. But we told him we'd be gone for a week."

"I wouldn't put it past your family to have the marina notify them when we left."

Kelly had to agree. Even so, Max could still be innocent of any wrongdoing. What sane man, if he was wanted by the law, would volunteer to go back home with her when he knew her brother was a suspicious policeman?

She told herself she could trust Max, that he was brave and heroic enough to rescue an animal he had no use for. Honest and honorable enough to keep a promise even if he suspected he might be walking into trouble.

A loud clap of thunder shook the car. Lightning flashed across the horizon. Sheets of rain pounded on the windshield and obscured her vision. Kelly stirred uneasily and turned on the windshield wipers. "I hate thunder and lightning," she muttered as the rain increased. "I can't even see the highway clearly."

When another lightning bolt lit up the sky, Max peered out the window. "Maybe we ought to stop here for the night."

Kelly breathed her relief. Thank goodness they weren't going home to a small, single bed. "Where's here? If it has a roof, four walls and a bed, I'm game.''

''A motel called My Blue Heaven,'' he answered as he peered out the window. ''That's a laugh, when everything around here has turned midnight-black. I can't see a whole lot more, but the way the storm is picking up, I definitely think we ought to stop.''

''Good enough.'' Kelly pulled into the motel parking lot where neon lights flickered with each new bolt of lightning.

''Hi, folks,'' the owner said cheerfully when they dashed in out of the rain. ''The storm sure has brought a lot of you people in here tonight. Got only one single room left, but it's yours if you want it for fifty dollars. Of course, it'll be five dollars extra for the dog.''

Max ignored Kelly's whisper for him to ask for two beds. He dug into his wallet and handed the man his credit card. ''We'll take it.''

''You folks on your way to Las Vegas to get married, are you?'' The clerk reached behind him and turned on the No Vacancy sign.

''Not exactly,'' Max answered. He nudged Kelly in the ribs when he heard her draw a deep breath. ''Why?''

''Because the room you just rented is our honeymoon suite,'' the clerk said happily. ''We're right proud of it, too. You'll see.'' He handed Max a room key. ''Number 12. Right off the highway, nice and quiet.''

''Great.'' Max reached for the key. ''Does it have a telephone?''

''Sure thing. The cottages were built forty years

ago, but I'm sure you'll find everything you need," he added proudly. He gazed at Max. "Say, you'll have to come through the switchboard if you're planning on making any telephone calls. We charge two dollars a call, unless it's long-distance. You can only call those collect. Don't want to be stuck with any big phone bills." The clerk frowned.

"No problem," Max assured him.

"Right. I expect you folks will be too busy to do much phoning at that," the clerk added, his good humor restored. His meaningful gaze rested on a dripping Kelly. "Want me to come with you and turn on the electric wall heater?"

"No thanks, I'll take care of it." Max grabbed Kelly by the arm. "Let's go, sweetheart," he said as he made for the door.

"They call this a bridal cottage?" Kelly shuddered when she and Max came into the cottage and he turned on the lights.

Max came up beside her, dropped their suitcases on the floor and looked around. He had to smother a grin. The entire room, including the ceiling, was painted blue. The double bed was covered with a floral purple and green bedspread to match the drapes. A distressed maple nightstand stood on one side of the bed, a television stand and a vintage TV on the other. An iron coffee table sat in front of a red leather couch. A telephone stand stood beside it.

The only concession to married bliss was a dried floral wreath over the bed.

Through an open door, he glimpsed an ancient bathtub. "It's not in the same league as the Majestic," Max agreed, "but since I don't see any water stains on the walls, I'd say it has a solid roof and four walls.''

He saw Kelly eyeing the leather couch. ''Stop right there,'' he said. ''I'm not sleeping on a couch again.''

Kelly glanced over at the bed. ''The bed's only a double. How are we going to fit?''

''It's a big improvement on your bed at home,'' Max answered firmly. ''And if having me so close bothers you, we can bundle.''

Kelly counted the number of pillows. ''Bundling might work. And don't forget Honey.''

''Bundling it is,'' Max said ruefully. Even in his condition, the idea of holding Kelly in his arms sounded just like what he needed. ''As for the mutt, she sleeps on the couch.''

He took off his wet coat and reached for the telephone. ''Now that that's settled, it's a good time to make those telephone calls. Especially to Bennett. If he has the marriage certificate, we can pick it up in the morning.''

A series of lightning flashes lit up the room, followed by loud cracks of thunder. Honey yelped in alarm and jumped into Max's arms. The lights went out.

The way his luck was running lately, Max knew the electric wires and telephone lines had been hit by lightning. He said a prayer and reached for the phone. Sure enough, his bad luck held. The phone line was dead.

''Max?'' Kelly's frightened voice sounded in his ear. ''Are you still there?''

''Unfortunately, yes,'' he replied, groping in the dark for Kelly. ''All things considered, I'd much rather be at the Majestic where they have auxiliary generators. Where are you?''

''Here,'' Kelly answered, bumping into him with a thud. ''Good, you've got Honey. What are we going to do now?''

''Wait it out, I guess,'' Max answered as he gathered her in his arms. He paused for a moment as a thought hit him. Maybe his luck was turning. ''I don't think the electric wall heater is going to work either. A better idea would be if we undressed and got into bed to keep warm.''

''Are you sure about the heater?''

''All the electrical lines are probably down, or the lights would have come back on by now,'' Max assured her. He groped for the edge of the bed. ''I don't know about the two of you, but I'm for bed.''

Kelly listened for the rustle of Max's clothing as he undressed. When his shoes hit the floor, she heard him mutter softly. ''This sure has been one helluva honeymoon.''

She repressed a giggle and considered whether or not to join him. A new series of lightning flashes and thunderclaps made up her mind. ''Wait for me,'' she said hurriedly. ''I'm coming to bed, too.''

She peered around her. ''I can't see my suitcase to get my nightgown.''

''Improvise,'' Max's voice sounded in the dark.

''Improvise,'' Kelly repeated under her breath. Her whole life the last few days was one improvisation after another. She undressed to her underwear and crawled under the cold blankets with Honey. ''Good heavens, it's freezing in here!''

''Come over here. I'll warm you up.'' Max pulled

her into his arms. "And as for you," he told a shivering Honey, "you're on your own. Find your own bed warmer."

As if she understood that Max was talking about her, Honey burrowed her way under the blankets to the foot of the bed.

"Wait a minute! You said we'd bundle if we had to go to bed together."

"Yeah," Max agreed. "But that was before the storm hit and the lights went out. And since the electric heater won't work, not to mention the telephone, I figure these are extraordinary circumstances."

After a few moments, Kelly whispered, "I'm still cold. Can I come closer?"

Max groaned. "Sorry, you're going to have to lie still, or I can't take responsibility for what might happen next."

For a full moment, there was a deep silence. "What happens now?"

"Are you sure you want to know?" Now that his seasickness was over, Max didn't know whether to laugh or groan over his sexual frustration. Driven by her fear of the storm, Kelly was asking a lot of a real man. Being honorable, he couldn't take advantage of Kelly's fright. He closed his eyes and concentrated on being noble.

Maybe it was the storm raging outside that frightened her, or the fact that Max had nothing on but his boxer shorts, but Kelly couldn't seem to get close enough to him. As a child she'd hidden under the bed during a thunderstorm rather than be laughed at by her older brothers. Hiding under the bed tonight was out. Tonight she wanted Max's warmth, the comfort of his arms. She wanted him to make love to her and to protect her from her fears.

"Yes," she answered, snuggling closer. "I'm sure. We can bundle later."

Chapter Seven

Max was sure his self-control was being challenged. His body demanded passionate sex, but he knew in his heart that Kelly deserved more tender loving.

The first time he'd made love to her the night of his cousin's wedding, they'd both been lost in a romantic fog. Lost, perhaps, but somehow precious memories managed to persist.

He couldn't recall the details, but he could remember how uninhibited they both had been. Tonight was a different story. Tonight, she needed more than loving, she needed his protection.

He wasn't sure about the approach he should take. If he bombed out, so be it.

His testosterone level urging him on, he tried a different strategy. He could always back off if Kelly changed her mind. "Even though we're not on the base, maybe it would be more fun if you pretended to be my wife."

"Pretend to be your wife?"

"Yes. I'm sure you used to like playing pretend when you were a little girl."

"Well, yes," she said, sounding puzzled. "But what does that have to do with tonight?"

"No buts," Max answered, a finger on her lips. "Just listen for a minute. Here's what I suggest we do. We'll pretend we're newlyweds, together for the first time. We can play Twenty Questions so I'll be able to find out what you like best about being married. You can pretend there's only us—the world is out there and we're alone in here. How does that sound?"

He could almost hear the wheels spinning in Kelly's mind as she thought about his proposal.

"Okay," she finally answered. "I'll try anything if it makes me feel warmer."

Max closed his eyes and blessed nature for the storm going on outside. And the one that was building inside him. "We'll both come out ahead, I promise." He kissed the nape of her shivering neck. "We can settle the subject of our actual marital status later."

Before the glow of marital bliss could grow cold, Max leaned over the edge of the bed to where he'd dropped his slacks and groped in his pocket for his wallet. Thankfully, he'd had the foresight to replace his protection when he'd shopped at the marina market. He hadn't known how Kelly would see their honeymoon status, but he'd hoped for the best. And tonight, he vowed, as he settled next to Kelly, tonight *was* going to be the best—for both of them.

He took Kelly into his arms. "Ready to pretend?"

Kelly knew the sexual attraction between herself and Max was still alive. What had started out as a lovers' game of one-upmanship was fast turning out to be the real thing.

Not that she knew much about him yet. He was great at rescuing dogs and great in bed, but that was about it. Too bad she hadn't paid more attention when DeeDee had prattled on and on about him.

There was one more thing: she knew Max was a man who lived by agendas. A man who could be as controlling as her father and just as chauvinistic as her brothers.

The truth was, she was actually growing fond of Max. As for loving him, she was getting close. But marriage was something far in her future, if at all. In the meantime, there was something more immediate for her to think about.

"Okay, you win," she said. "But just for tonight."

"Tonight," Max agreed. He ran his strong hands over her back. "We've got to get rid of this," he murmured. He unsnapped her bra. "And this," he added, helping her slide off her bikinis.

"I've never felt so cold," she whispered, shivering in his arms. "Are you sure you can't turn on the heater?"

"Sorry, the electricity is out," he murmured, "but I'm sure I can take care of that in a minute."

He kissed her cold shoulders again, then down her satin skin to the curve of her hips. "Getting warmer?"

"A little." Her voice was breathless, she shivered under his hands. "What's the next question?"

"I'm a great believer in show, don't tell." Max smiled and renewed his efforts. Her hips were next. He rubbed her waist, the sides of her hips, until her body warmed under his hands. "How's that?"

"Much better," she answered with a contented sigh. "What's the next question?"

"This." Pleased with Kelly's uninhibited response, he laughed and nuzzled the inside of the thigh that had worn the bridal garter.

"Much better," Kelly answered over her shoulder. "Maybe we don't need the rest of the Twenty Questions."

Max chuckled and turned her over to face him. The lightning flashes that lit up the room showed him green eyes wide and warm with passion, and nipples hard with desire.

"You're right," he said as he moved over her. He held her face in his hands and they traded a deep kiss that sent his senses reeling.

"Mmm...I don't think I need to worry about a wall heater anymore," he heard her whisper. "How about you?"

Max laughed deep in his throat and renewed his efforts.

Under his hands Kelly felt good and somehow right. Her tiny gasps of pleasure sent pangs of answering excitement through him. Whatever else was wrong with their relationship, this undeniable attraction they felt for each other wasn't one of them.

"Wrap your legs around me and let me warm the rest of you," he whispered.

The storm raging outside forgotten, Kelly followed his coaching. Each kiss, each touch, each whisper heightened the pleasure building around her. Soon, they were a single cocoon wrapped in each other's warmth.

"Warm enough now?" he whispered in her ear.

"Not yet," she answered faintly, "but I'm getting a lot warmer."

All her nerve endings cried out for relief from the forces growing inside her. Moved by the feel of him, the taste of him, she buried her face in Max's shoulder and nibbled at his salty skin. She was shaken by his touch, the sound of his voice. With each burst of pleasure, her fears were forgotten. Max was a man who was taking her out of the storm's darkness and into a world of light and loving.

"I'm warmer, too," she finally heard him answer as he shifted above her. All thoughts of why she needed him tonight forgotten, she gave herself up to her surging need. Behind her closed eyes, pleasurable sensations swept her. His skin slid across hers until the dark room seemed to erupt in a burst of flame.

"Kelly," she heard Max say as he kissed her one last time and fell to his side with her in his arms. "I've never known anything quite like this, nor anyone like you." His skin damp with effort, he brushed her hair from her forehead and hugged her close. "Are you okay?"

"Very," she answered, fitting herself to the curve of his body. "You were right. You're much better than a heater."

"Still want to bundle?" She heard him laugh.

"No way," she answered, too sated, too warm and too sleepy to move. "Don't move until I tell you to." As far as she was concerned, she was content to stay in Max's arms until the storm outside and within her passed.

THE MORNING SUN streaming through the window brought Kelly partially awake. Aware of every part of her body, and too sleepy to let her dream go, she sank back into an erotic dream in which Max had loved and warmed her throughout the night.

She thought back to DeeDee's wedding, and Max's insistence that that night had been their wedding night, too. At the moment, she felt so much at peace with the idea, she was beginning to wonder if he was right. She couldn't imagine making such tender and passionate love with anyone but a man she loved deeply—Max.

She noticed he was gone when she glanced over at the untouched pillow beside her. She thrilled to remember how they'd spent the night sharing her own single pillow. She remembered his strong, muscled arms. Lean demanding legs. Hard lips that had sought and plundered her mouth.

"Rise and shine!" The words were followed by a kiss and the aroma of coffee tempting her nose.

"Max?"

"Who else were you expecting?"

"I don't want to get up," Kelly smiled into the pillow that carried Max's masculine scent. She burrowed into the worn mattress. "I could stay here forever."

"So could I, but..."

"But what?" Kelly squinted up at Max. He was standing beside the bed, a thermos in one hand and a brown paper bag in the other. His eyes were dancing with mischief, and something more. It was the something more that made her body tingle.

She sat up and thrust the erotic pictures out of her mind when her stomach growled. With electricity restored, the wall heater hissed and groaned. Grateful for the sharp, rich aroma of freshly brewed coffee, she took the cup Max handed her. "Where did you find coffee in this nowhere place?"

"Believe it or not, the motel clerk sent a thermos along as part of the amenities that come with the bridal cottage," Max answered with a wry smile. "I'm afraid he didn't offer much more. Only these." He handed her a chocolate doughnut in a plastic bag. "The guy said he'd heard chocolate is an aphrodisiac, but added that I looked as if I hadn't needed any help."

"Oh my God," Kelly moaned, rubbing her bruised lips. "What we did last night must be written all over us. What will people think when we get home?"

"Not to worry," Max answered cheerfully. "As long as your father thinks we're married, he's probably passed the news on."

"Yeah," Kelly muttered. But somehow that didn't make her feel any better. She searched beneath the blankets with her toes. "Honey's gone! What did you do with her?"

"Nothing as bad as what you're thinking," he answered with a grin. "I figured the bed was no place for the three of us, so when you fell asleep I wrapped her in our coats and put her on the couch."

Kelly searched the room over the rim of her paper coffee cup. "Where?"

"I didn't have the heart to wake you this morning so I took her out for a walk before there was a problem. Right now, she's on a leash outside the door until it's safe to bring her inside."

Kelly frowned. "How come I don't remember any of that?"

"You were sleeping too soundly." He took her empty coffee cup and put it on the nightstand. "You know, at first I thought this place was the pits, but I'm actually beginning to grow fond of it. How about you?"

Kelly gazed around her. The garish too-purple and too-green drapes and the antiquated furniture were still there. But they somehow looked softer in the early-morning sunlight. Nothing about the room could compare to the bridal suite at the Majestic, but after the night they'd enjoyed there, she loved it too. Not that she'd admit it. "The biggest thing this place has going for it is that it doesn't move."

"I don't know about that," Max answered playfully. He sat down on the edge of the bed with a broad smile. "I swear it was moving last night."

Kelly felt herself blush. She thought of the number of times she'd wound up in Max's arms. After DeeDee's wedding, a night together in a bed she'd outgrown years ago and the near miss on the boat, it had taken a storm to send her into his arms. If it had been fate, fate must have been working overtime.

She studied his warm brown eyes, square jaw and athletic body she'd come to know so well last night. He was all male, from the grin that curved at his lips to the leather sandals he wore on his feet. And, to her surprise, she was actually beginning to like having him around.

"Like the old saying goes, it's okay as a place to visit," she finally answered with a grin, "but I wouldn't want to live here."

He laughed. "Kelly O'Rourke, you are one of a kind." He brushed her cheek with the back of his hand and caressed her with his eyes. "Do you think you could stand staying here a little while longer?"

Kelly warmed. She would never need artificial heat as long as she was around Max. "When is checkout time?"

"Whenever we're ready to leave. And if it costs a few more bucks, it'll be worth it. Maybe the clerk will throw in lunch."

Max was joking, but the look in his eyes told her he was in no hurry. Neither was she. "How about Honey? She needs to be fed."

"No problem," he answered. He hooked a finger over the blanket that covered her, slowly drawing it down to her waist. "I left her a chocolate doughnut. The last time I looked, she seemed happy enough."

"Dogs aren't supposed to eat chocolate," she protested, momentarily diverted from his long, sensuous fingers and the promise in his eyes. "Sugar gives dogs worms."

"Tell it to the mutt," he answered as he bent over and blew gently on the sensitive spot between her breasts. "She thinks she's human, anyway. Besides, when she smelled the doughnuts, she sat up and begged for one."

Kelly sighed and reached for the top button on his shirt. "I can see you're going to teach her bad habits."

"Unless I miss my guess, I'm sure she already knows all about bad habits." He captured her hands in his. "First, tell me who you are this morning? Mrs. Taylor or Miss Kelly O'Rourke?"

"Ask me later," she answered, drawing him down to meet her lips. He guided her fingers through the opening on his shirt with a low, satisfied groan. "Nice," she whispered. As she ran her hands over his skin, felt his muscles tighten.

"Better take it easy," she heard him say in a shaky voice. "I'm not sure how much of this I can take. Leave enough of me to return the favor."

"Go ahead," she invited, busy with the remaining buttons on his shirt. "I dare you."

"Better be careful," he cautioned. He caught her busy fingers in his hands. "Remember, I'm a sucker for a dare."

"So am I." Kelly kissed him below the chin. "When do we start?"

In moments, the blue room, Honey, and the world outside the cottage vanished.

"READY TO GET UP, sleepyhead?"

Kelly felt so comfortable and fulfilled, she definitely wasn't ready. She opened her eyes. Max was up, dressed again and ready to leave. Their wonderful night was over, the strong sun shining through the window brought reality with it. "I guess so," she answered reluctantly.

She gazed up at Max and actually resented his good humor. Here she was still basking in erotic dreams and his mind had moved on. Just like a man. "What are we going to do now?"

"*You're* going home." Max handed her her clothing. "As soon as I've gotten you settled in, I'm going to the nearest telephone and try to get in touch with Troy. Then I'm going to the Majestic to find out the name of the minister who married all of us. And then there's Bennett. If he can't produce our marriage certificate, I'm going to tackle the marriage-license bureau." He shrugged into his jacket and raked his fingers through his hair. "There has to be a record of our wedding somewhere."

Reminded that she and Max might not be married after all, Kelly sobered. Had she made a mistake when she'd given herself permission last night and this morning to love Max?

Judging from the uncertainty in Max's voice, she realized she'd been right to hesitate to commit herself to being Mrs. Taylor beyond last night. Even after a night of making love, Max had turned out to be as controlling as the rest of the men in her life. Last night, the thought of being truly married to him had been growing on her, but today was a different story.

In the beginning, Max had seemed to respect her desire to want to make her own choices. He might have insisted they were married, but he *had* offered to help her strike out on her own. Whatever the reason he'd been so agreeable about going along with her until now, he was a different man this morning. Today he was determined to prove she was his wife.

When Kelly didn't take issue with him, Max studied her too-quiet expression. "What's up? Have you remembered something about the night we met?"

"Not really," she replied evasively. "I was just thinking that we could settle this sooner if I helped look."

"It would be more helpful if you went home and tried to find out where Troy and DeeDee are honeymooning so we can call them. They've got to know something about this wedding business.''

"I suppose you're right," she answered, flinging back the covers. She reached for her clothing and headed for the vintage bathroom. "Give me a few minutes to shower and dress."

Max smothered an impulse to join her in the shower. What was his rush, anyway? They *were* on a week's honeymoon, weren't they? He was about to match action to thought when he realized how important it was to search for the wedding certificate while the trail was hot. He didn't want Kelly to be the bride that got away.

"I'd better go check on the mutt," he called to the bathroom door. "By now, she's probably finished the doughnuts and is looking for seconds."

BENNETT'S SECRETARY looked up with a brilliant smile. "Why, hello, again. How have you and your new wife been doing?"

Max's spirits perked up. "You mean you remember me?"

She giggled. "Who could forget you?"

"Well, that's good, Miss Bailey," he answered, noting her nameplate. There was noise outside in the lobby, but the lack of activity in the office worried him. "Is Bennett in?"

"No. He's on vacation, hiking in the mountains somewhere up north."

"Hiking? Up north?" Max's spirits took a nose-dive. "Are you sure about that?"

"Yep," she said airily. "Reggie told me he's tired of living in a goldfish bowl and watching other people get married. He said he's going where there are no people, bright lights, slot machines or telephones. Is there anything I can do for you?''

"Maybe," he answered. He was about to sound like a fool, but he forged ahead. "In all the excitement, I forgot to pick up my marriage certificate. I was hoping Bennett had it."

"Not that I recall." A frown crossed her forehead. "Wait a minute, I'll check his desk."

His fingers crossed for good luck, Max heard drawers open and close in the adjacent office, then her footsteps approach. "Sorry, there's nothing of yours in there. I'm afraid you'll have to wait until Reggie comes back. You can ask him then."

Max mentally cursed the black cloud that hung over him. "When do you expect him back?"

"In about two weeks." She giggled. "He said if he's enjoying himself, he might just make it three."

"Thanks. I'm afraid even two weeks will be too late." He wiped his sweating hands on his jeans. "Can you give me directions to the marriage-license bureau?"

Miss Bailey gazed at him with a quizzical look. "Sure, but why would you want to go there? You're already married, aren't you?"

Noting her friendly interest, Max decided honesty was the best policy. "You may get a laugh out of this, but that's what I'm trying to prove."

"What's the matter?" Bennett's secretary laughed. "Too much celebrating to remember clearly?"

The last thing Max wanted was for the secretary to dismiss him as an irresponsible lush. "No, I think it was a case of getting carried away by my wife."

"In that case, sit down. Maybe I can save you a trip." She gestured to a chair and handed him a pen and paper. "Write down your name and your wife's maiden name. I have a cousin who works at the marriage-license bureau. Everything is on computer nowadays, you know. I'll call and ask Flora to run a check."

Max obliged. Anything to get at the truth.

Miss Bailey picked up the receiver and dialed. "Flora? This is Janet. Do me a favor, will you?" With one eye on Max, she went on to relay the information Max had given her.

Max slowly counted to one-fifty before he saw Janet frown at him. "Are you sure? There has to be some kind of record. I saw them get married myself. In fact, the guy's sitting right here in front of me." After a moment, she bit her lip. "Yeah, thanks. I owe you one."

Janet hung up the phone and frowned at Max. "Sorry. My cousin says you're not on the books. How come you got married without having a license?" She paused, leaned over the desk and whispered, "You might not even be married. Does your wife know?"

If Janet's cousin Flora was right, Max realized he might be home free. The big question was, did he want to be? "*I* know," he muttered, "and that's enough. The hotel wouldn't have allowed us to get married here if the whole thing wasn't on the up-and-up, would they?"

"Of course not. And certainly not with all the celebrating they had scheduled." She frowned at Max. "Whatever happened, it wasn't the hotel's fault. So don't think you can sue."

"I wouldn't dream of it," Max replied, standing up and backing to the door. How could he continue to be so unlucky when he'd actually counted on finding the certificate? How could he lose Kelly just as he was growing to care for her?

"The way things are going, I must be cursed," he muttered. For a guy who had planned his life to the last hour, how could he have wound up in such an unplanned mess? He turned back to where Bennett's secretary watched warily. "Whatever happens, I want you to know I'm grateful for your help."

UNABLE TO BRING HIMSELF to give Kelly the news that would free her, Max drove aimlessly. In the distance, the endless hard-packed brown desert, covered by mesquite and other desert shrubs, looked as cold and empty as his thoughts.

How could he accept the probability that he and Kelly weren't married when he was sure there had been a wedding ceremony? A ceremony Reggie Bennett, his secretary and the housekeeping staff had claimed they'd witnessed?

Sure, at the beginning of their relationship neither he nor Kelly had wanted to be married, not even to each other. But sure as hell, things had changed so fast he was almost speechless. In the space of four short days, Kelly's wry humor, her blithe spirit, her laughter and even her dog had gotten to him. And in the process, changed him.

The truth was, married or not, he hated to let Kelly go.

In spite of the wonderful night they'd just spent together, did he owe her the truth? Did he owe her the chance to pursue the freedom she'd said she wanted?

When he finally drove to the O'Rourke cottage, Max found a dozen cars parked around the house. Sure his bad luck was chasing him even now, he made his way to the front door.

At his knock, Sean threw open the door then hollered over his shoulder, "Kelly, your husband's here! Come on in, Max. You're just in time for the celebration."

Celebration? Max froze when at least twenty people, each holding a can of Guinness, turned to look at him. His heart sank, but he tried a feeble smile. There went his chance to have a heart-to-heart talk with Kelly. To tell her the truth, and then to ask her a few questions about how she saw their future.

Bowls of potato chips and popcorn were scattered throughout the living room. The scent of corned beef and cabbage filled the air. Honey, who was excitedly racing around the room begging for treats, headed for him the moment she spotted him.

Max had to smile when she jumped into his arms and licked his face. "Sorry. If you're looking for more chocolate doughnuts, we're all out." He folded her under one arm and turned back to Sean. "What are you celebrating?" he asked, as if he didn't know. Honey settled for licking his chin.

"Our wedding." Kelly hurried to his side and whispered a cautionary word in his ear. "We're having a special dinner to celebrate."

He studied her with disbelief. *Did* she want to stay with him? Go through another wedding ceremony, if necessary? He would have asked, but this was obviously the wrong place and the wrong time.

The scents wafting from the kitchen caught his interest. Maybe he'd been wrong about Kelly's culinary achievements. "Don't tell me you're doing the cooking?"

She smiled, pressed his hand and glanced at the kitchen. A heavyset woman with the trademark O'Rourke copper hair and a smile bright enough to light up the house was striding into the room wiping her hands on her apron. "Don't be silly. Aunt Brigid is making dinner. She lives near here, in Henderson. When she heard I was back home, she came right over to help us celebrate."

And, from the size of the crowd, if it hadn't been Kelly's father who'd spread the word, this Aunt Brigid surely must have called everyone she knew, Max mused silently, his teeth aching behind his studied smile.

"And why wouldn't I be here when my only niece has gotten herself married? I've given up on those two brothers of yours," she told Kelly with a disgusted look at Patrick and Damon.

Before he could blink, Kelly's aunt beamed at Max and gathered him in her arms. "And since no one around here knows how or cares to learn how to cook," she said with a reproachful glance at Kelly, "I'm making a grand dinner for the lot of you."

"What's for dessert? Aunt Brigid?" Sean, a can of Guinness in his hand came up behind her.

His aunt took the beer can out of the fifteen-year-old's hand and gave it to Max. "There's ginger ale in the kitchen for the likes of you," she admonished

Sean, prodding him toward the kitchen. "As for desert, there'll be a pudding if you behave yourself. You come with me and leave the drinking and celebrating for the grown-ups." She turned back to Max. "And as for you, young man, drink up. From the look on Kelly's face when she came home, I'd say you've earned one or two." She winked at Max and disappeared into the kitchen.

Embarrassed by the woman's provocative remark, Max smiled his thanks to the kitchen door. Privately, he wished he were anywhere but center stage in front of Kelly's family and friends. He and Kelly had a lot to talk about, but it didn't look as if they would be talking anytime soon.

"Uncle Jake, this is Max Taylor," Kelly announced to a big, burly man who made a beeline for her and Max. "Uncle Jake is Aunt Brigid's husband. And these are my cousins and family friends," she added as she led Max around the room and greeted each one by name.

Max felt his right hand grow numb from all the handshakes, his cheek red from all the lipstick kisses. He realized Kelly was a part of a large, affectionate family who loved her and whom she loved. Coming from a reserved family, he wondered if Kelly knew how lucky she was.

Now that their marriage was being celebrated in public, how could he tell Kelly the fruitless results of his search? He couldn't believe he'd dreamed he and Kelly had gotten married the night of his cousin's wedding, but how the hell was he going to prove it?

How could he tell Kelly the probable stage of their

relationship? How could he leave her to face her disapproving family alone?

What if he left her and went home, and her father's remark about consequences came true? No way! No matter what their marital status was, he cared too much about Kelly to just walk away and leave her.

But what would Kelly say if and when he *did* get around to telling her he couldn't find Bennett? Or that there was no official record of a wedding certificate? If there *should* be consequences, would she believe he'd made up the wedding ruse in order to con her into going to bed with him? Not once, but twice?

One way or another, he was going to have to be Kelly's husband for the foreseeable future.

Chapter Eight

Kelly made her way back to Max's side with a fresh tray of canapés in her hands. "Try one, I helped Aunt Brigid make them." She glanced around to make sure they couldn't be overheard. "We need to talk. I have information for you," she added under her breath.

Max checked the tray that was clearly the extent of Kelly's culinary efforts. He reached for a peanut butter and jam–covered cracker and smiled at her when his hand brushed hers. Her answering smile sent sparks of an electrical awareness through him.

The expression on her face told him she was on to something. A good something? He fended off Honey who was nibbling at his shoe.

Kelly laughed at Honey's antics, leaned down and fed her a plain cracker. "Maybe we ought to go to my bedroom?"

"Our bedroom, you mean, don't you?" Kelly looked so damn appealing, he couldn't help making the question hot and sultry.

Kelly returned his smile, but she wasn't laughing anymore. "You might say so," she answered. "At least, as long as everyone thinks we're on a honey-moon.''

Max gave up and fed his unfinished cracker to Honey. ''What happens next?''

''We can talk about it later.'' She took a quick glance around the room. ''The aunts have a romantic look in their eyes. They think we're on a honeymoon. We can't disappoint them, can we?''

Max had to hand it to Kelly. With a few key pro-vocative words, she was able to make his body tem-perature rise. But her look spoke of something else besides a honeymoon. Had Patrick beaten him to dis-covering the status of their marriage? Was it too late to tell her the truth?

''Lead the way,'' he answered with a glance around the room. Kelly was right. The aunts were gazing at him with stars in their eyes. Now that introductions and congratulations were over, the men had returned to discussing the merits of Guinness over domestic beer. At the rate cans of Guinness were being con-sumed, the Irish beer was winning, hands down.

On the other hand, Kelly's father stood watching the proceedings with his arms folded across his chest. Beside him, Father Joe was deep in thought. Their body language didn't look promising.

To complicate matters, Max could see Patrick and Damon eyeing him. Damon's speculative gaze kept drifting to his sister, while Patrick had that piercing lawman's look aimed right at him.

What if the two men had been comparing notes while he and Kelly were off attempting to honey-moon? Had Damon told his brother he suspected Kelly's marriage wasn't on the up-and-up? Had Patrick beaten him to the marriage-license bureau? Put together, the answers to the questions that spilled across his mind spelled trouble.

The threat on their faces was too real. If subsequent events revealed he and Kelly weren't legally married, his face was going to wind up on Patrick's wanted poster. WANTED: MAX TAYLOR—SEDUCTION OF KELLY O'ROURKE.

Still Max remained dumfounded by the case of the nonexistent license. Not only because Bennett's secretary had told him she'd seen him marry Kelly, but because his own memory was slowly returning. Sure as hell, some kind of marriage ceremony had taken place between Kelly and him. Troy's return from his honeymoon and Bennett's return from his vacation became more vital than ever. Max took a last swallow of beer and calmly returned the O'Rourke brothers' scrutiny.

He fixed a firm eye on Honey. "No more crackers, and leave my shoes alone!" Honey sat on her haunches and wagged her tail. Ready to swear the mutt had actually grinned at him, Max gave up and let the standoff pass.

Kelly reached for her pet. "She knows a softy when she sees one. You might as well let her come along. She won't give us away."

"I don't know about that," Max answered with a disgruntled look at Kelly's dog. "She has a mind of her own." With Honey victoriously wagging her tail, he followed Kelly into the bedroom.

"I have DeeDee and Troy's telephone number!" Kelly announced when Max closed the door behind them. "DeeDee's mom gave it to me. I told her how important it was I speak to them and she told me they're in Fiji, at the Turtle Island.''

"Thank God!" Holding the telephone number, Max could see the end of his search for proof of his marriage to Kelly. His heart pounded with excitement as he studied the slip of paper. He glanced around the small bedroom. "No telephone?"

"No. Dad figured the one in the living room was enough." She paused for a moment, deep in thought. "As soon as we can get away, we can go and use the telephone at the officers' club."

"Okay." Max thought of all the unexpected problems that had plagued him since his arrival. This was one more. "Maybe it's just as well. Your dad would have questions if he saw long-distance calls to Fiji on his phone bill."

Just once, he thought grimly, it would be nice if he could reach the bottom line about this marriage business without having to go through an obstacle course. So far, time and events had kept him from finding the answer he needed; Kelly's brothers, the lack of a working telephone on the boat, at the motel in Boulder City and now. And then there was Bennett's vacation. With the storm, even nature had conspired against him.

Of course, their brief sojourn at the My Blue Heaven Motel had made up for a lot. Under other circumstances, he wouldn't have minded staying there another few days exploring a future with Kelly. Instead, he was here surrounded by a crowd of her relatives all interested in his honeymoon. He added the current lack of privacy to the string of bad luck that was apparently dogging his heels.

Gazing at the worry lines that appeared on Max's forehead, Kelly was troubled. She was still trying to get over their short stay at the motel in Boulder City, without much success. Every thrilling moment with Max replayed across her mind. Max seemed to have dismissed it.

A feeling of disappointment ran through her. Surely the way Max had made love to her must have meant as much to him as it had to her. "Are you sorry about all this?"

"No, can't say that I am." He put the slip of paper in his shirt pocket and smiled ruefully. "To tell the truth, I have to tell you these past four days have been some of the most interesting days of my life. How about you?"

Interesting? The last of Kelly's golden glow dimmed at the question. This was the first time she'd heard making love referred to as "interesting."

She took a deep breath. If he was playing a game, two could play. "I'm fine," she answered lightly. "After all, when you take a dare, you have to be prepared to pay the consequences."

She glanced down at Honey who was watching Max with worshiping eyes. What did Honey, or herself, for that matter, know about the real Max anyway?

Maybe she'd been foolish in thinking there was a special bond between them. Just as well she'd found it out now, before she gave her heart away.

Max, torn between the way he had begun to feel about Kelly and his possibly thwarted plans for the future, forced himself to smile. Maybe he'd misread the look in her eyes and in her touch when they'd made love earlier.

He could have sworn that somewhere along the line their lovemaking had become much more than a game. Or had it merely been because of the storm raging outside the motel's honeymoon suite?

She didn't act as if she felt he'd taken advantage of her. Maybe it was just as well. He needed time to find himself, to decide what he really wanted out of life.

One thing he was sure about now. A future with Lian was out of the question and he intended to tell her so. Since they'd practically been raised as siblings, surely she would understand.

Now, the remaining problem was the definition of "consequences." In Kelly's language and in her father's, consequences were definitely not the same thing. For Kelly's sake more than his, he hoped Kelly's interpretation was closer to the truth.

He took a careful look at Kelly. The teasing glint in her eyes was gone, and so was the woman who had made passionate love with him. Maybe now was the time to talk about the future. "Kelly, I think we have to talk about where we're going with this."

He was interrupted by a loud banging on the door. "Hey, you guys! Aunt Brigid said to tell you dinner is ready. And to remind you that you two have the next fifty years for that gooey kind of stuff!"

Kelly flung open the door. "Sean O'Rourke, you know darn well Aunt Brigid didn't say that! Especially in your hearing!"

"You're right." Sean backed away into the living room and grinned mischievously. "All she talks about in the kitchen is babies. But I figured this was the only way to get the two of you out here. You can make out later. The rest of us are hungry.''

Heads turned at Sean's comment. Hands holding cans of beer froze in midair. There were nervous giggles in the background.

Uncle Jake guffawed. As if his laughter was a cue for the assorted aunts, uncles and friends, they all broke into laughter. ''He's got you there, Kelly!'' Uncle Jake roared. ''My niece is a true Irishwoman,'' he announced proudly. ''Warm-blooded. When she gives her heart to the man she loves, she goes all the way. Just like my Brigid.'' He beamed at the kitchen door. ''And I have six strapping sons to prove it.''

Kelly glowered at her uncle. Just once, she would have liked not to be teased or tormented just because she was the only girl in a family of boys. Just once she would have liked to be treated as a grown woman with a mind of her own. Teasing her may have been funny when she was a kid, but it was time for everyone to realize she wasn't a child anymore.

''Uncle Jake,'' she warned, ''this isn't the time or place for such talk. I'm not ready for a family!''

''Don't take me wrong, lassie,'' he replied, surprised at her reaction. ''I've teased you since you were a wee bit of a lass.''

''Well, I'm not a wee bit of a lass anymore,'' Kelly retorted. ''I'm a married woman and I'm entitled to a little decorum and respect. Especially since my husband is here.''

To her satisfaction, Max reached for her hand. She needed all the moral support she could get.

''Decorum? Respect?'' her uncle echoed. ''How

about love? To most of us, you're still the wee one in this picture I've carried since the day you were born.'' He pulled out his wallet, took out a snapshot and proudly handed it to Max. "Take a look at this. Would I be carrying this around with me if I didn't love the lass?''

Kelly looked at the snapshot in Max's hand taken in the tradition of earlier times; a little baby, nude on a fur rug.

"Oh my God!" she muttered. She grabbed the snapshot out of Max's hand and held it out of her uncle's reach. "No way do you get this back unless you promise never, ever to show it to anyone again.''

"This one ought to please you," Jake went on. He extracted several snapshots and handed one to Max. "That's Kelly and her first boyfriend.''

"Uncle Jake," Kelly said testily, "if you don't put the pictures back in your wallet, I'm out of here. And Max goes with me!''

Aunt Brigid stormed out of the kitchen in time to hear Kelly's warning. "Jake O'Bannion, mind your manners. What are you doing to our Kelly?''

"Ah well," her uncle muttered, glancing at his irate wife. "Sometimes a man can do with a few less good women in his life.''

"It all depends on who's the woman," Max answered, drawing Kelly to his side. "I'm going to keep this one.''

Kelly held her breath. Not too long ago, she would have been annoyed at Max's announcement of ownership, but not tonight. Tonight, she needed to belong to someone who would stand up for her as a woman, not a child.

Aunt Brigid nodded her approval. "Jake," she said pointedly, "you might take a lesson or two from our Kelly's man."

Her husband snorted. "So tell me, me boy, just what is it you do that will keep our Kelly and your children in grand style?"

"Uncle Jake, stop that," Kelly protested. "It's no one's business what Max does for a living but mine. As for children, there aren't any."

"Not yet," her uncle answered, giving Max an approving once-over. "But from the looks of the man, it's clear it won't be long before a bairn or two is on the way."

"Uncle Jake!" Kelly gasped, red-faced. "I told you—"

"That's okay, I don't mind explaining." Max soothed. "Actually, Mr. O'Bannion, I'm into physical fitness."

"And that you are," Jake said approvingly.

"And you look physically fit to me, too," Aunt Brigid remarked. She started to reach for Max's arm. Two of the aunts moved forward to follow her.

Kelly stepped in front of Max before her aunt connected with his arm. "Aunt Brigid! Aunt Clara! Aunt Lily! Not you, too!"

"I was only going to feel the man's muscles," Brigid protested. She headed for the kitchen in a huff. The other two aunts nodded in unison. "Us, too," Lily commented with a knowing smile. "The man looks willing enough."

Kelly had visions of other members of the party lining up to test Max's physical fitness. Mindful of the quantity of beer the guests had imbibed, she didn't intend to start a riot. She settled for waiting until her aunt shook her head and headed back into the kitchen.

"Being into physical fitness is a fine thing, me boy," Uncle Jake went on. "But tell me, what is it you do for a living?"

Before Kelly could stifle her uncle again, Max hurried to answer. "Have you ever heard of Taylor Fitness Centers?"

"Ah yes, the gyms back East," Jake replied. "I've been in one of them a time or two. Do they belong to you?"

Max nodded. "I'm thinking of opening another one here in Las Vegas."

Jake eyed Max with approval. "No wonder you're such a braw laddie. Maybe that's why our Kelly's so attracted to you. She teaches aerobics on the base, did you know?"

"Yes," Max glanced appreciatively at Kelly's trim figure. "That's why she looks so good to me."

Kelly grabbed Max's elbow before her uncle could elaborate on her employment. "Come on, Max, let's get back into the kitchen. Aunt Brigid wants us to make a taste test."

"The woman is more likely to ask you when she can expect her first great-niece," her uncle called after them. "Lately, she's been saying this family needs a few more girls to even the score. Not that the good woman is offering to make a contribution herself, you understand." He glanced at the kitchen door. "I'm afraid she's run out of steam."

Kelly gritted her teeth and pulled Max after her.

"Why the bum's rush?" Max inquired when they were out of her uncle's hearing.

"Because my uncle was about to launch into a speech about a woman's place being at home with kids, that's why," she replied. "I've been listening to that line ever since I was a thirteen-year-old tomboy. Becoming an aerobics teacher is the closest I could get to living in a man's world without my uncles and Dad going into a tizzy."

"Ah, there you are." Aunt Brigid beamed with approval when Kelly and Max entered the kitchen. "I was just thinking that you and your fine young man would make fine parents."

Kelly rushed to forestall any remarks about babies. "Aunt Brigid, we came to help out. That's all."

Aunt Brigid looked disappointed. "Well, then, you're just in time to put these on the table. Kelly, you can carry the soda bread and the relish tray. Max, you carry the corned beef and cabbage." She handed Max a heavily laden platter.

Almost blinded by the steam rising from the platter of corned beef and cabbage, Max followed Kelly back into the dining room. A happy roar went up from the crowd. "Here's to the newlyweds!" someone shouted, hoisting a can of beer. "May they enjoy each other for a hundred years."

"And here's to my Brigid, God bless her," Jake added. "And to the next generation of O'Rourkes!"

Kelly put the bread on the table and threw up her hands in surrender.

For Kelly's sake, Max smothered a smile. She might be annoyed, but he was impressed by the amiable display of affection. She'd been on the receiving end of more love in a few short hours than he'd experienced in a lifetime.

He watched while guests vied for helpings of corned beef and cabbage and boiled potatoes. Cans of Guinness were raised with each boisterous toast to himself and his bride. In his view, Kelly looked as if she wished she were someplace else, but he was enjoying himself.

Thank goodness his own mother and father weren't here, he thought with a guilty start. His mother would have been overcome by the free and easy conversation, his father would have lectured him for an hour over the evils of liquor. The only one who might have appreciated the raucous scene would have been his sister, Jeane. She still managed to have a sense of humor, despite having been raised in a series of girls' boarding schools. In a way, she reminded him of Kelly.

He glanced over at Kelly. In spite of the way she felt about the attention she was getting, she was trying to be a good sport. He listened to her bandy words about with her uncle, watched her hug her aunts and try to keep a mischievous Sean in line. A beautiful blithe spirit, she was so different from Lian. Lian was a woman from his own background—and just as steeped in agendas.

"Everyone is so busy trading stories, I think we can sneak out for a while," Kelly whispered when she eventually made her way back to his side. "We can go over to the officers' club and be back before anyone realizes we're missing."

"You're sure? After all, this party is for us."

"I'm sure," she answered firmly. "Come on, let's take the back door out of here before someone comes up with another story to embarrass me."

Max grinned. "I find it kind of interesting."

"I don't. So, do you want to go and make the phone call, or don't you?"

"I do," Max said, his attention brought back from his perusal of Kelly's luscious lips to the reason he had to get in touch with Troy. "Let's go."

The officers' club was jumping.

"Over here," Kelly gestured to a telephone mounted on the wall.

"Is this the best we can do?" After a good look at the activity surrounding them, Max despaired of ever having a private moment to make his telephone call. But he was too close to finding out the truth to give up now. He took his calling card out of his wallet and placed the call.

Between the static on the line and the noise surrounding him, Max could barely hear the Fiji hotel telephone operator come on the line. "Mr. Troy Taylor, please." He waited impatiently for his cousin to answer. "Thank God," he said when he heard his cousin's voice. "Troy, it's Max. You've got to help me. I'm in big trouble. I have to know what went on the night you and DeeDee got married!"

There was a pause. "No, I don't remember, or I wouldn't be calling you!" Max shot Kelly an exasperated glance. "Start at the beginning," he went on. He put a finger into one ear to close off the noise. "Yeah, yeah. I remember that part. The part I don't seem to remember is if, when and how Kelly and I wound up getting married ourselves!"

Trying to overhear the conversation, Kelly moved closer to Max until she was leaning on his shoulder.

To her dismay, a shout went up at the table nearest
them.

"Hey, Kelly, hear you got yourself married last
weekend. Looks as if you can't keep your hands off
the guy. How come you haven't introduced us to the
groom?"

"We've been busy," she shouted back. When her
friends broke into laughter, she realized how intimate
she and Max appeared. She started to pull away, but
Max's free arm snaked around her shoulders and drew
her back. There was more laughter. Cheerfully waving at her audience, Kelly heard Max shout into the
telephone, "Troy! Are you there? Troy! Can you hear
me?"

"Damn!" Max finally swore and slammed down
the receiver.

"What's the matter?"

"I don't know." Max frowned at the telephone.
"A bad connection, I guess. All I could hear was
static. Hang on while I try again."

A second try reached the hotel operator in Fiji.

The noise surrounding Max continued unabated.
"What do you mean there's no answer?" he hollered
into the telephone. "I was just speaking to Mr. Taylor
a minute ago! How about sending someone up to ask
him to call me back at this number?" He gave the
operator the number on the telephone he was using.
"Thank you. I'll wait right here for his call."

"Max?"

Max tried to control his frustration. "Something's
gone wrong at the other end," he replied, raking his
fingers through his hair. "I asked the hotel telephone

operator to have Troy call me back. In the meantime, we'll have to wait here.''

"Oh no," Kelly said in mock horror. "As soon as everyone sees you're off the phone, they'll be after us to join the party."

"That's all I need. Another party." Max raked his fingers through his hair again.

"Most of these people are my friends. It wouldn't be polite to ignore them."

"Lead on, then. If you can take it, I guess I can, too."

Before Max knew what was happening, someone thrust a drink in his hands and he was accepting congratulations for winning the hand of the prettiest redhead on the base. Kelly seemed to be taking the situation with good nature, but then no one was flashing a snapshot of her bare butt on a fur rug.

An hour later, Troy still hadn't returned the call. Kelly was making signs that it was time to go back to the party at her home.

"We'll see you folks around." Max waved goodbye to Kelly's friends. He drove back to the O'Rourke celebration deep in thought. He'd put so much hope in Troy telling them what had really happened at the Majestic wedding ceremony. He was still in the same quandary: no license…but an eyewitness. There was still a possibility Kelly was his wife. But if it turned out to be true, would a marriage between them work when they were so obviously two different people and so obviously belonged in two different worlds?

Kelly wanted freedom of choice. Taking her home as his wife wasn't it. Back home in Boston she would be bound by the same conventions he was accustomed to and had only lately found confining. If his mother had her way, she would turn Kelly's life into an endless series of programmed cultural and charitable events, just as she had her own. Even Lian had been raised in the same blue-blood first-family traditions.

He tried to think objectively about Lian. After meeting Kelly he realized he couldn't live with a woman like his mother. Nor could he accept the kind of life he would have to live with Lian.

One thought led to another. He was struck by the realization that his life had actually been planned *for* him instead of *by* him since the time he was a small boy. His life had been orderly and predictable. Looking back, he wondered how he'd managed to put up with it.

Knowing the kind of life waiting for Kelly, would it be fair to take her home with him? The answer came like a lightning bolt. Unless he could find a way to turn his life around and live the unstructured life Kelly dreamed of, he had no right to contemplate life with her.

In the light from the car interior he glanced over at Kelly who, in the space of a few days, seemed to have become part of him. Asleep against his shoulder, she felt soft as down. Small sighs escaped her parted lips that reminded him of the blush color of the Zinfandel wine they'd shared back at the officers' club. He felt an unfamiliar tug at his heart and felt closer to Kelly than he'd ever felt to another human being.

Judging from the snapshots her uncle had shown him of a youthful Kelly, she'd grown into a lovely, if headstrong, woman—just as her father had remarked. Not that he blamed her. She'd waited a long time for the chance to escape to a different kind of life than the one she had.

He felt a deep regret for the trick fate had played on them both. Meeting Kelly had changed him forever. As for Kelly, she deserved more than a man who wasn't sure about the direction his life would take from now on.

As soon as they could find some time alone, he intended to be honest and up-front with her.

Whatever she was looking for, a future with him wasn't it.

Chapter Nine

Max's decision to leave tomorrow reluctantly made, he drew up to the O'Rourke home.

"Kelly?" Max shook her gently. "We're home."

She awakened with a start, straightened up and yawned. "So soon? I was having a great dream."

He smiled and brushed a coppery strand of hair away from her expressive hazel eyes. He wished he could remain a part of her life, but the reality was they hardly knew each other. And what he did know about Kelly told him he owed her the chance to make her dreams come true. Even if they didn't include him.

"I guessed as much from the smile on your face," he said tenderly. "In fact, I've been driving around for the past twenty minutes to give you a chance to catch up on your sleep."

"Thanks. I am exhausted." She yawned again and stretched. "Two parties in one night are more than I can handle. Thank goodness I don't get married every day."

Max hid a rueful smile. With Kelly playing marriage tag, he was never quite sure just how she saw their relationship. "My guess is that the parties aren't the only problem. I'm afraid I didn't give you much of a chance to sleep last night."

Her eyes twinkled back at him. "What makes you think I wanted to sleep?"

Her appealing smile sent his senses into a tailspin. If they hadn't been parked in her driveway, he would have taken her up on her dare. "That's my girl!"

She caught her breath. *Was* she his girl? In spite of his laughter, she'd sensed an uncertain undercurrent in his voice. Aware of him in ways that went beyond the physical, her heart began to beat faster. Her gaze locked with his.

He was a strong yet tender lover. Protective and good-natured in a situation that would have sent any other man rushing for the nearest exit. But not Max—he'd stayed to watch over her and protect her from gossip.

And yet, she wasn't sure she could share her thoughts with him. To tell him he was the man who kept appearing in her dreams, both now and back at the My Blue Heaven Motel. That, awake or asleep, she couldn't get him out of her thoughts.

She studied Max's solid profile. By now, she felt so attuned to him, she was able to sense there was something different about him tonight.

"You look as if you want to tell me something," she said quietly. "Something you don't think I want to hear." As much as she'd hoped she was wrong, when the look in his eyes sobered, she knew she had been right. "Now that we're alone, you might as well tell me what you're thinking."

"You're right. Although I was hoping it could wait until everyone is gone and we're alone."

Kelly shook her head. "There's no telling how long the party will last. Once we go into the house, we won't have a chance at privacy."

Max hesitated for a long moment before he steeled himself to tell her what was on his mind. "I hope you won't misunderstand what I'm going to say."

"Try me." A cold sensation ran through Kelly. Her happy dream faded. Something *was* wrong, and it wasn't his unfinished telephone conversation with Troy.

He started to reach for her hand, then drew back. "To begin with, I think—no, I know I owe you an apology. Everything that's happened in the past few days has been my fault. If I hadn't gotten carried away by a misplaced sense of humor at Troy's wedding, we wouldn't be in this mess."

"It wasn't all your fault. I'm afraid I was more than a little impulsive, myself."

"That's the point, Kelly. You may be the impulsive type, but I'm not." He brushed her cheek, so tenderly she wanted to turn her lips into his hand. "Maybe it was because you were so irresistible that night. I should have known better than to take you up on your dare."

"I couldn't help it," she confessed with a rueful smile. "It's the Irish in me."

He took her cold hand in his. "Anyway, before I go any further, I want to tell you I wouldn't trade these past few days with you for anything."

"Me neither." Kelly felt a hollow pit forming in her stomach. Max was saying goodbye. She felt as if she were poised over the edge of an abyss and that a slight wind could push her over. She swallowed hard. "But nothing lasts forever, does it?"

In the bright lights coming from the kitchen windows, she saw him bite his lower lip. Whatever his reason for saying goodbye, it obviously wasn't easy for him.

"No, I'm afraid not," he said in a voice tinged with regret. "The truth is, you told me you wanted out of here, that you weren't ready to be a wife. I know I haven't been much of a help to you—instead, I've stood in the way of your finding and living your dream. The way I see it, without me, you'd stand a fighting chance. But don't worry. I promise to talk to Bennett and get to the bottom of our situation."

She started to protest. He put a forefinger to her lips. "Let's face it. As much as I'd like to stick around, I think I owe it to both of us to move on."

Her heart aching, Kelly could feel his regret, read it in his eyes. How could she tell him, or herself, he was too late? That she'd already found her dream, even if it wasn't the dream she'd set out to find?

"I'm afraid I'm not the right kind of a guy for you," he continued into her silence. "You need a man who shares your desire for a new life. Unfortunately, my life is marked by agendas. Now that I've met you, I hope to do something about that. Until then I've responsibilities at home to take care of. But before I leave, I owe you a wedding ring."

Kelly shook her head. "You don't owe me anything. I'm a grown woman, in spite of the way my family sees me. I can take care of myself. I should have told you so before now. As for a ring, it would be premature if we're not going to go through with the wedding ceremony Dad's planning.''

''A ring would keep your family off your back until we're sure you're not pregnant. If not, we'll find a way to quietly break off the marriage. As for the ring being premature, we've been premature about a number of things, so why should we stop now?''

Kelly felt a warmth seep through her as she thought about the ''number of things.'' The way he'd gazed into her eyes, held her in his arms, kissed away all doubts and fears. And about the splendor of their joining. ''Things are different now.''

''Not so,'' he answered. ''I owe you a wedding ring. More than that, I owe you the truth about our marriage. I want you to pick out a ring tomorrow. And, unless you want to do the research yourself, I'll find out about the missing marriage certificate as soon as I'm able to come up with a few answers.''

Kelly shook her head. She could hardly keep up with Max's reasoning. But one thing was crystal clear. Max was saying goodbye.

Because of her father's military career, she was used to goodbyes. She'd cried more than once over leaving friends as a youngster. This time, she would say goodbye no matter how much it hurt. And before Max had a chance to say it first. ''Let's be honest, Max. You're moving on. That's what this is all about, isn't it?''

''Yes, I'm afraid it is. But I still want to give you a wedding ring to wear while I'm gone. Like I said, you can wear it until you find out if there are any consequences.''

His wry smile almost broke her heart. How many

men would willingly face up to the responsibility of fatherhood if they didn't have to? But more to the point, how could he have made such passionate love to her knowing he intended to leave? How could he deny the wonderful attraction that existed between them?

She blushed at the memory of last night. "I don't think we have to worry. At any rate, I plan on leaving here next week. Dad will never know."

"You're sure?" He looked so concerned about her he almost broke her heart.

"I'm sure," she answered with a certainty she was far from feeling. She had to lie. How else could she let Max go? She smothered her tears. No matter how things were shaping up between them, she wanted to take that worried look from his eyes. She owed him that much. After all, she was just as responsible for what had taken place the night they met as he was, wasn't she?

"In the meantime," he said, "I have a plan."

"Not another plan," she protested lightly to mask the ache in her heart. "Your first plan hasn't done too well."

"Better than you seem to think," he answered. "Your dad seems satisfied."

Kelly's eyebrows arched. "Because we spent a night here before we went off on a honeymoon Dad planned? Knowing him, I don't think so."

"No. Because, man to man, I promised to bring you back here and I have. As for the rest, what with my getting seasick and the storm that sent us home, I'm afraid it wasn't much of a honeymoon, was it?"

Kelly considered everything that had happened

since they'd met. There was the wedding night they'd spent together at the hotel. There was their houseboat honeymoon and Max's heroic efforts when he'd saved Honey. There was the exchange of inner thoughts that had helped her to get to know him. And there was the wonderful, sensuous night at the My Blue Heaven Motel when she'd fallen in love with him. Memories she would treasure forever.

As for being home free, that was another matter. She could take care of herself without Max. But there *was* the possibility of a baby. And Patrick to contend with. If Max only knew, once her brother got the idea Max might be on a wanted list, Patrick wasn't the type to give up. Ever.

"You know, in spite of his blustering, your father has a way about him," Max said with a rueful smile. "And so does the rest of your family. I wouldn't deliberately do anything that would hurt any of you."

Kelly shrugged. "It doesn't matter. I intended to leave, and I still do."

"It matters to me," Max answered. "I suggest you postpone your plans and stick around here for a while. No, don't shake your head. I know I'm right. We can tell everyone I've been called back to Boston on business. That'll keep things quiet for a while. If it turns out we're actually married and…expecting, you can quietly file for divorce on the grounds of desertion."

"It's not as though I want to be married," she protested. "I know I agreed to act married as long as we're here on the base, even if we can't be sure we actually are. You haven't been able to come up with any written proof."

"I'm going to find the proof eventually. It's just a

matter of time. Until then, I think we should act married, on the base or not.'' A burst of hilarity from the house distracted Max. ''Sounds like things are winding up. Maybe we'd better go on in.''

With an annulment now out of the question, how could she remind Max that in a family like hers divorce was impossible? Even if she'd grown weary of tradition and wanted a new life, she couldn't bring herself to be the first to break her father's heart. Would her freedom be worth it?

It might be different if Max wanted her for herself, and not because he felt he owed her or for a baby's sake. She might even have become used to the idea of being Mrs. Maxwell Taylor, of actually marrying him. But, considering what he'd just said, she wasn't going to have the chance to try.

''You can quit worrying, Max. Haven't I been telling you all along you have nothing to worry about?''

''Maybe, maybe not,'' he answered. ''But there *are* people who say they saw the wedding ceremony. As for my finding proof, Troy and DeeDee are going to come home eventually, and so is Reggie Bennett. In my opinion, we have to go on being married for a while.''

Kelly fought back her tears. No matter how he sugarcoated their situation, Max was saying goodbye. She nodded her agreement.

''Good. So this is what I suggest we do. We'll keep the 'maybe' out of this and assume we're husband and wife. If it turns out you *are* expecting, we can go through another marriage ceremony and take it from there. To please your father, we can invite everyone, my family included. Until then, all we can do is hope everything turns out all right.''

He sounded satisfied. She wasn't.

Under any other circumstances, Kelly knew she would have been happy to have Max's child. But not now. Not when he was proposing a future with his fingers crossed.

''Whatever you say,'' she answered, vowing never to give her heart away so easily again. She reached for the car-door handle. ''We'd better go in now before someone comes out looking for us.''

''Patrick, for instance?''

Kelly's hand froze on the door handle. ''What makes you say that?''

''Easy.'' Max shrugged fatalistically. ''I've seen the way he keeps watching me. Can't say I blame him. I'd be pretty curious about a stranger my own sister brought home. Especially if she announced she'd married him.'' His eyes narrowed as he studied her. ''I can tell by the look on your face you know something I don't know. Right?''

She did. And, as much as she loved her brother and honored his profession, she cared for Max too much to let him take a fall—especially if he wasn't guilty of anything. She took a deep breath. Her goodbye present to Max would be to warn him he was in jeopardy.

''Were you ever in New Jersey?''

''New Jersey?'' Max's mouth fell open. ''What has that got to do with anything?''

''Plenty. Pay attention. So, have you?''

''Lots of times,'' Max replied. ''I have a chain of centers in Atlantic City.''

Kelly's heart sank. "Have you ever been arrested there?"

"Arrested? You've got to be kidding!" He peered at her as if he was convinced she'd lost her mind. "Out with it. What the hell does New Jersey have to do with me?"

"Just this. Patrick thinks he's seen a New Jersey wanted poster with you as the star attraction."

Max burst into laughter. "He's got the wrong man. I'm so damn clean I squeak." It took a few minutes before he could stop laughing. "What is the guy wanted for? Murder?"

"No," she answered solemnly. "He's a con man. I heard Patrick tell Dad the guy made a practice of picking up women in the gambling casinos."

"So just because you picked me up in Las Vegas, I'm supposed to be the guy?"

"I wouldn't exactly say *I* picked *you* up," Kelly retorted. "I definitely remember it was mutual."

"Okay, okay," he answered impatiently. "So it takes two to tango. Go on."

"Patrick said you have a strong resemblance to the guy in the wanted poster. He was going back to his office to see if he could find the poster again. Knowing my brother, he's already done that."

Max grimaced. "So I was tried and convicted on a series of circumstances even before I had a chance to prove my innocence?"

"It's partly your fault. You refused to give Patrick your social security number. Maybe he had no choice but to believe you were hiding something."

"Ah yes. My social security number." He gazed at the house. "At the time, I couldn't help myself. I thought it was a hell of a request and I lost my temper. After all, you introduced me as your husband. That should have been enough for him.''

''All the more reason for him to be worried.''

His face inscrutable, Max looked at her. ''I don't give a damn about what your brother thinks, Kelly. What I want to know is do *you* believe it?''

She wanted to tell him she cared too much for him to believe he could be a con man. She'd trusted her heart to him before, could she do it again? ''I'm not sure I know what to believe in anymore.''

Before Max had a chance to answer, the kitchen door opened and Patrick strode to the car.

''Where have the two of you been?''

''We went over to the officers' club,'' Kelly replied when she saw Max clench his hands and grit his teeth. ''I wanted to introduce Max to some of my friends.''

''It could have waited until tomorrow,'' Patrick retorted, his eyes on Max. ''Better go on in, Kelly. You're just in time to say good-night to everyone.''

When she started to protest, Max reached over and opened the car door for her. ''Go on, Kelly. Everything is going to be okay.''

She glanced at her brother, then at Max. Things didn't look too promising. ''Are you sure?''

''I'm sure. I'll be in in a minute. Your brother has a few things to say to me and he might as well get them off his chest.''

For Patrick's benefit, she kissed Max on the cheek. ''Stay cool,'' she murmured in his ear.

''I'll try.'' He squeezed her hand reassuringly. ''Go on in.''

Max waited until Kelly was in the house before he

got out of the car. "I take it you wanted to talk to me?"

"Frankly, yes," Patrick agreed. He eyed Max with a practiced, professional eye. "I did some investigating at the Las Vegas marriage-license bureau while you and Kelly were away on your honeymoon." His voice took on an edge. "I didn't like what I discovered."

Max knew his only chance was to forestall what was coming next. "If you're trying to tell me you couldn't find any evidence of our application for a wedding license, or a record of a marriage certificate, I know all about it."

"The hell you say!"

"Yeah. You'll have to believe I'd never do anything to hurt Kelly."

"You can say that again!" Patrick glared and looked ready to take him on. "You'll hurt Kelly over my dead body!"

"Cool it, man! I've already said I'd never hurt her. You're just going to have to take my word for it."

Max couldn't tell Patrick about the obstacles he'd encountered trying to untangle his marriage to Kelly. Not without giving away her warning, or the possibility she was still single. He couldn't tell Patrick he intended to be on his way soon, maybe forever. What would happen if Kelly turned up pregnant and unmarried?

Patrick's body language spoke volumes. Max decided it would be wise to compromise. "I figure you have your reasons for being worried about Kelly. I have a sister myself. So, if you still want my social security number, you've got it. But that's all."

Patrick grimaced, his gaze steady and sure. "I'm going to take you up on that. But I want you to know that it's not so much the law I'm worried about, it's our Kelly. We all love her too much to see her get hurt."

Max gazed over Patrick's shoulder at the kitchen door. He could make out the shadow of Kelly's silhouette behind the window, watching, waiting. He felt a tug at his heart. "I told you, I don't intend to hurt Kelly."

Patrick exploded. "Man, you're playing with my sister's life! What are you going to do about it?"

"Lower your voice, please. If you keep this up, Kelly's bound to come back out here. I promised you I wouldn't hurt Kelly, and I won't. It's just that I have to leave, for now, anyway. I've business affairs waiting for me back home to tend to." He looked Patrick straight in the eye. "I swear to you I'll come back if Kelly needs me. For anything." He emphasized the word *anything*.

Patrick didn't look convinced. "Kelly's been saying she wants to quit her job at the gym and go out on her own. What if she decides to do it while you're gone?"

"No matter. She'll tell me where to find her."

Patrick's eyes bored into Max. "Okay, but only for Kelly's sake. But you'd better be on the up-and-up or *I'll* find *you!*"

"I am. I swear it."

"We'll see. Now, as for Kelly, as much as she seems to resent us, Dad, Damon and I have always kept an eye out for her for her own good. Sean too," Patrick added wryly. "That is, if he lives to grow up.

At the rate he manages to shake up Dad, there are times when I doubt it. He's so much like our Kelly when she was younger, it's scary. And I want you to know that as long as she's here, we don't intend to stop keeping an eye on either of them.''

Max held out his hand. ''I'm on your side.''

Patrick shook his hand, reluctantly, it seemed to Max. ''For now.'' He sighed. ''Maybe we'd better go on in. It's time to say good-night to the family. We can talk again later.''

When he followed her brother into the house, Max nodded to a hovering Kelly. She smiled her relief. ''Uncle Jake says he's not going anywhere before he gives you some words of advice. Try not to laugh.''

Geared up for another lecture, Max followed her into the living room. Uncle Jake was waiting for him.

''Ah, there you are.'' He sized up Max. ''Man to man, just a word to the wise,'' Jake announced solemnly. ''The O'Rourke women are a strong-minded bunch. 'Tis their red hair, you know,'' he added confidentially. ''And the fact that there seems to be so few of them in the last few generations. Spoiled, the lot of them, I tell you. Including my Brigid. You have to be firm.'' He took a quick glance at the kitchen door. ''But with you being so physically fit and all, you might want to be careful.''

''I wouldn't harm a hair on Kelly's head,'' Max assured him with a straight face. ''I've found a kiss usually ends an argument.''

''You don't say?'' Jake looked pensive. ''Too bad my Brigid doesn't stop talking long enough anymore for me to try it.'' He sighed. ''Of course, when we were younger...'' His voice trailed off reflectively.

"Well, now that bit of advice is out of the way, I think I'll seek me bed. Brigid, me love," he called. "Are you coming?"

"I'm right here, you big ox." She thrust a package at him. "Lunch." She caught Max to her ample chest. "Take good care of our Kelly. She's more precious to us than you know."

"I will, Aunt Brigid," he vowed and returned her hug.

One by one, the remaining guests dropped words of wisdom as they said good-night. By the time the last door closed behind them, Max could hardly restrain his laughter. God bless the Irish, he thought affectionately. They had more vintage advice than the minister at his church back home.

He gazed at the departing O'Rourkes. He was used to living an uninteresting life; hadn't even realized how dull he and his own family were until now. Troubled, he watched Aunt Brigid gather Kelly in her arms to say good-night. He heard her aunt's booming words of advice, and Kelly's answering laughter. How different everything was from his own home and formal family gatherings.

The realization reinforced his belief that Kelly wouldn't fit into his family any more than he could fit into hers.

Patrick hovered beside him. When Max turned to look at him, the man raised an eyebrow. Damn! He'd promised Patrick his social security number. Better to give it to him now before he asked for anything else. "Be with you in a minute."

He went into Kelly's bedroom to retrieve a business card. As he was writing down the information

Patrick had requested, he glanced at the narrow bed he had shared with Kelly. It still looked too small for comfort, he mused, but tonight was his last chance to be close to Kelly before he left.

He put the pen aside and contemplated the bed with a wistful smile. He relived the too-short night he and Kelly had spent in there together. A night when her sweet scent had kept him awake long after she'd finally fallen asleep in his arms.

It had been a night when he'd begun to realize how much he'd grown to admire her spirit. To care for her, and to marvel how she seemed to inspire love and affection. The night at the My Blue Heaven Motel came to mind.

He remembered how Kelly seemed to belong in his arms.

He was torn between his duty to Kelly and his certainty she would only be unhappy with his life-style back in Boston. He couldn't stay around here and ignore his business interests, either. Sure, he had employees to take up the management slack when he was gone, but that was another story. He knew he had to go back to Boston soon, even though something inside him urged him to stay and keep Kelly safe.

At the same time, he knew Kelly would only resent one more male watching over her out of a sense of duty. She may have taken his decision to leave stoically, but he'd seen a sadness lurking in her eyes. Torn between his resolve to leave and his desire to stay, he felt like a heel.

He finished writing down the information Patrick wanted. There was no use dwelling on his decision.

He'd already said goodbye. He couldn't put Kelly through that twice.

In the end, his decision to leave without spending this last night with Kelly was taken out of his hands.

"Now, back to basics," Michael O'Rourke announced when the door closed behind the last celebrant. Father Joe, the only remaining guest, nodded his agreement. The senior O'Rourke cast a stern look at Kelly. "I expect you and your husband to start talking with the father here early tomorrow morning about a proper marriage."

Considering she and Max had just decided to come to a parting of ways, Kelly was speechless. She glanced at Max for a cue.

Max stepped into the conversation. "Sorry, sir, I thought I'd told you before. I don't have any more time to spend here. I have an urgent business issue back in Boston."

Michael O'Rourke's face reddened with anger. "What more important business is there than my daughter getting properly married?"

Used to giving orders, Kelly's father had resorted to his standard military operating procedure. He may have phrased his words as a question, but from the look in the man's eyes and his body language, Max took it as a command. It was going to take all his diplomatic skills to back out of this without causing Kelly any more grief.

"I'm sorry, but remaining here is out of the question. I have a family back East who doesn't know where I am. And there's my business interests to take care of."

"You should have thought of that before you and

Kelly decided on this foolishness!'' O'Rourke glared at him. "I don't see why you're concerned about your family at this late date. After all, *I* had to find out about your wedding on television!"

"Dad!"

O'Rourke shook off Kelly's hand. "Your place is here, taking care of our Kelly!"

Kelly's face mirrored her frustration. "I can take care of myself, thank you! I've known from the start that Max had to go back East."

Father Joe intervened. "A minute, Michael. I have a question for Kelly." He turned to her. "And why is it you can't go with your husband and meet his family? Of course," Father Joe amended after a hot glance from Kelly's father, "maybe it would be better if you both left for the East *after* you have a proper wedding."

Max sensed Father Joe was sympathetic, if not wholly on his side. "Because we thought it was only fair to give Kelly a chance to get her affairs in order first," he answered. "To give her a chance to get used to the idea of a different life in new surroundings, with people she doesn't know. In fact—" he turned to Kelly's father "—I thought you would appreciate having Kelly remain here with you for a time."

"The young man makes sense, Michael," Father Joe announced after a few seconds' contemplation. "There's no use rushing into things. Is there?" His question was directed at Kelly.

"No, Father," Kelly answered. "And Max is right. I could use a chance to get used to the idea."

Father Joe smiled benevolently. "With a young man like your Max waiting for you, child, I have a feeling the two of you will be back together sooner than you think."

Chapter Ten

Father Joe had warned it wouldn't take long for Max to miss Kelly. He'd been right. It hadn't taken him more than a few hours. She'd gotten into his blood. And now those hours had stretched into a week.

Max stared at the calendar on the wall. How could a woman he'd known for such a short time have become a vital part of him?

His thoughts were in turmoil. Without Kelly, his arms felt empty, his body ached with longing. He missed her teasing smile, her sense of humor, her sparkling presence. He even missed Aunt Brigid and Uncle Jake and the bevy of O'Rourke relatives. And someone else he hadn't anticipated missing—the dog, Honey.

He couldn't concentrate on business. His friends had remarked on how antsy he'd become and wondered aloud what was up. His mother had blamed it all, testily, on a missed Hawaiian vacation. His father had taken him aside and told him forcefully it was time to get serious.

At the thought of his parents, Max sighed. Now that he was able to view his life from the outside looking in, he realized his life-style hadn't been of his own making. Instead, he'd been groomed from childhood to follow his father's footsteps in the health food business. The only time he'd deviated from The Plan had been to establish the successful Taylor Fitness Centers. And only after his father had grudgingly agreed.

He'd had enough. Even if he came off as a fool, it was time to take charge of his own future. A future with Kelly as his wife. Provided she was willing to take the plunge with him.

His decision made, there was still his relationship with Lian to settle. A duty he wasn't looking forward to. But decency and honor called.

When Lian had taken him aside and tactfully asked if he was telling her the whole truth about what had kept him from meeting her in Hawaii, he'd stuck to his story about business in Nevada. He hadn't had the heart to tell her about Kelly. Until now.

Just as he'd mistakenly felt he'd owed Kelly the truth about how he viewed the future of their relationship, he owed Lian the truth about theirs.

He reached for the telephone and made an appointment to meet her for lunch.

"Max, darling!" Lian met him inside the entrance to her favorite restaurant, threw her arms around his neck and kissed him soundly on the mouth. "I had a feeling you wanted to speak to me."

Max forced a smile and gently untangled himself. "You're right." At the restaurant owner's effusive greeting he realized inviting Lian to meet him here where they were both well-known had been a mistake. How was he going to explain to Lian he thought of her as a sister or a friend after a greeting like this?

"How about lunch before we talk?" he said.

Lian pouted, but good-naturedly followed the maître d' to a table. "I'm really not hungry," she announced as she sank into the chair he held for her. "Coffee and a fruit salad would be fine. Actually, I'm too excited to eat. I can't wait to hear why you asked me to meet you here in our special place."

From the bright look in Lian's eyes, Max realized she was expecting him to propose. "In a minute." He gestured to a waiter and ordered coffee for two, Lian's salad and a club sandwich for himself. That done, he drew a deep breath and plunged into the misadventure in Las Vegas that had turned him into a married man. For Kelly's sake, and to spare Lian's feelings, he omitted Kelly's possible pregnancy.

Lian sat speechless, her hand frozen on her coffee cup.

"Go ahead, call me a heel, a jerk, anything you want to," Max said when he ended his story. "I guess I deserve it for letting you believe I was going to ask you to marry me. The truth is, I've decided to go back to Las Vegas and settle the marriage-license issue once and for all."

"Go back to Las Vegas?" She looked at him blankly. "Are you sure you know what you're doing?"

"About as sure as I can be under the circumstances."

"How does Kelly feel about it?"

"I'm not sure, but I can hope."

''I take it I'm out of the picture regardless of the outcome?''

Max shrugged helplessly. ''I'm sorry, Lian… What can I do to make this up to you?''

She waved his comment away. ''I was so certain you were about to ask me to marry you. That's why I thought we were going to Hawaii together.''

Max's heart sank like a lead balloon. Lian was right. He *had* been about to ask her to marry him. More because she had become a fixture in his life than because he loved her. ''I'm sorry, Lian. I wouldn't deliberately hurt you, and yes, there may have been an understanding of sorts. I'm sorry.''

Lian bit her lip. He could see she was fighting back tears. ''Are you sure you love this Kelly of yours enough to win her back?''

''Yes. I hadn't realized how much until an hour ago.'' He forced a laugh. It sounded hollow, even to him. ''I must have been out of my mind to walk away from Kelly.''

Tears glistened in Lian's eyes at his answer. He felt like a bigger heel than ever, but at least he was an honest one.

She took a deep breath. ''I'm glad you told me now, instead of letting me make a fool of myself. I was actually starting to make wedding plans. I wish you and Kelly all the best. You know I've always cared a lot about you.''

''And I care a lot about you, too,'' Max replied. He felt guilty, yet relieved now that his possible marriage was out in the open. ''But now that I've met Kelly…''

Lian waved away a waiter hovering to refill her

coffee cup. "Do your parents know you may already be married?"

"No, not yet. Not when I'm not sure myself. I'd appreciate your not telling them until I'm ready." He smiled ruefully. "Who knows, Kelly may have written me off or filed for divorce by now."

"Divorce?" Lian looked surprised. "Why not an annulment? After all, you told me you only lived with her for a few days."

Max hesitated. "I know, but after…" Embarrassed, he left the sentence unfinished.

"Oh?" Lian blushed. "Perhaps you'd better not wait any longer. Go after Kelly before you lose her." She dropped her napkin on the table and rose to her feet. "But I want you to know I'll be here if things don't work out."

Max walked her to the door, returned her goodbye kiss and stood looking after her. Lian was right. He had to get back to Las Vegas ASAP.

HE TOOK A DAY FLIGHT to Las Vegas, first-class. Intending to be wide-awake and sober when he landed, he passed up the endless supply of cocktails and liqueurs. When he told Kelly how he felt about her, he didn't want her to think it was another case of jet lag or liquor talking. One way or another, he had to convince her he was sincere. Even if it meant taking her back to the privacy of the My Blue Heaven Motel for another honeymoon.

He signed for a rental car and headed out the highway to Nellis. The immediate problem was how to get into the air force base without giving Kelly advance notice.

Damon! That was it, he'd try to reach Kelly's brother. He hoped the guy would see things his way without putting up an argument or another obstacle. He'd had enough problems to last him a lifetime. One way or another, he intended to see Kelly. He'd come too close to making her his to risk losing her now.

He drove up to the entrance to Nellis Air Force Base where a vintage airplane and an enlisted man guarded the gate. "I'd like to see Lieutenant Damon O'Rourke, please."

The guard nodded politely. "Would you mind showing me your identification and stating your business, sir?"

"My name is Maxwell Taylor. I'm the lieutenant's brother-in-law." Max flashed his driver's license. The young guard lost his official look. "Kelly's husband?"

"You know my wife?"

"Sure, I take her aerobics class at the enlisted personnel's gym. Half of us guys were in love with her before we heard she got herself—" He caught himself and blushed. "Sorry, but seeing as how you're Kelly's husband, I guess I shouldn't be telling you that."

Max smothered a grin. "That's okay. Kelly does have that effect on people."

Relieved, the guard rushed on. "Funny thing though, when we tried to congratulate her, she didn't want to talk about it." He eyed Max curiously. "Sure you don't want to see your wife instead of her brother?"

"Not just now," Max confessed. "I want to surprise her. How about Lieutenant O'Rourke?"

The guard pointed to a parking lot just inside the gate. "Sure thing, sir. Why don't you park right over there while I contact the lieutenant?"

Max waited impatiently, debating how Kelly's older brother would receive him. By now, the guy would be either curious or angry enough to come to the gate to confront him. Hopefully, he would only be curious. Not that Max cared. He had the ammunition stashed in his pocket to convince Damon of his sincerity.

Convincing Patrick or his father might be a different story. But either way, no matter what, making his case with Kelly came first. He studied his wristwatch and got out of the car. Considering how Damon had looked the last time they'd met, he'd give the guy five minutes to get here.

A green military jeep pulled up, well within the allotted five minutes. An irate Damon hopped out and confronted Max. His voice dripped icicles. Before Max could speak, Damon punched him in the nose.

Max staggered against his car. Stars were floating in front of his eyes, bells were ringing. He straightened up and ducked the next punch.

"Hey, hold up a minute! I was hoping we could talk!"

"Talk?" Damon held up his fists, ready to strike again. "All I want to know is where in the hell have you been and what are you doing here now?"

Max saw the guard take a step toward him. He waved him away, pulled a handkerchief out of his pocket and wiped away a trickle of blood oozing out of his nose. "Can we go somewhere more private and talk?"

"No," Damon retorted. "After what you did to Kelly, unless you have a damn good excuse for being here, you're going no farther than this gate."

Max felt the blood drain from his face. *What he did to Kelly?* "Look. I'd hoped to do this without an audience," he said, gesturing to the watching guard, "but I suppose now is as good a time as any."

Damon's eyes narrowed. "For what?"

"For this." Max reached into his pocket and drew out a small blue velvet jewelry case. He opened the cover and turned the box toward Damon.

"An engagement ring?"

"*And* a wedding ring." Max waited while Damon's angry expression lightened up. "I saw the question in Patrick's eyes the morning after Kelly told you all we got married. I figured it was about a missing wedding ring. It was only a matter of time until I could answer your question." Max snapped the case shut and put it back in his pocket. "I wanted to show you all I mean business before Kelly found out I was here. No use my asking for trouble, or is it too late?"

Damon gritted his teeth and clenched his fists. For a moment, Max wasn't sure if the guy was going to hit him again.

"I don't know," Damon finally answered. "It may not be that easy. Pat's still checking you out. In fact, he told me you and Kelly may not be married. Are you?"

"God, I sure hope so," Max replied. "I'm here to find out."

"Pat hasn't said anything to Dad yet. As it is, Father Joe is trying to keep him from going after you with a shotgun. As for Kelly, she's not talking."

Max gingerly prodded his nose. Thank goodness it wasn't broken. "Look, it may take some doing, but I intend to fit all the missing pieces of the wedding puzzle together as soon as I can find them. All I need is to be given a chance."

Damon looked undecided. "I don't want Kelly hurt any more than she already is."

"Me neither. You've got to believe I care too much about Kelly to want to hurt her. But if you let me talk to her, I swear that before I'm through, I'll get everything straightened out. If it's the last thing I do."

Damon still hesitated, but Max was relieved to see him unclench his fists. "How do I know Kelly wants to see you?"

Max was ready with the answer. "Has she been her old self since I left? Has she mentioned me?"

Damon shook his head. "No. I told you, she's not talking to anyone. Dad's furious."

"Then the way I see it, you have nothing to lose by taking a chance on me."

"Okay," Damon agreed reluctantly. "She's at the gym, but I'm going with you. Just in case. If you cause Kelly any trouble, I might be the one to shoot you."

"Only as far as the door, if you don't mind," Max answered stubbornly. It was a trait he'd learned from his Irish bride. Besides, he wanted Kelly's undivided attention. "This is a private affair."

Max's heart pounded while he and Damon traded hard stares. The guy wasn't willing to give an inch, but he wasn't either. To his relief, Damon finally signaled the guard. "Okay. Leave your car here and hop in the jeep. I want you where I can keep an eye on you.''

THEY CAUGHT KELLY just as her aerobics class was ending.

Max's heart leaped into his throat. And not only because Kelly made such a lovely picture in lime green tights covered by an abbreviated flowered leotard. Because he loved her!

Although she looked thinner, her curves were just as he remembered. Her copper hair was bound back into a ponytail that took a few years off her age. She was dabbing at her throat with a towel and waving goodbye to the men and women in her class. She looked up and smiled when she heard his and Damon's footsteps echo in the large hangar-like gym. Until she realized he was back.

Damon stopped at the entrance. ''Okay, go ahead. I'll stick around long enough to make sure Kelly wants to see you. If not, you're outta here.''

''And if she does?''

''Then I'll leave.'' Damon's eyes took on the color of cold steel. ''But make no mistake, I'll be right outside this door. I shouldn't be in the enlisted personnel's gym, anyway.''

Max's eyes were on Kelly. ''Good enough. And thanks.''

He slowed his steps. He wanted to rush across the wooden floor, gather Kelly in his arms and show her how much he'd missed her. The few men and women who lingered stopped him. With each deliberate step, he expected Kelly to turn her back on him or head for an exit door. Her expression was wary, but he recognized an involuntary warmth that came into her eyes. Good.

"What are you doing here?" Kelly asked defiantly when Max came to a stop. "I was doing okay without you."

"I knew *you* would," he answered with a smile, "but *I* wasn't." He put his hands in his coat pocket to keep himself from reaching for her. He didn't mind waiting. There were a few things to settle before he kissed her doubts away.

Kelly slung her towel around her neck and took a step backward to keep from moving into his arms. Max's unexpected appearance and the crooked smile she thought she'd never see again were enough to take her breath away. "Why have you come back?"

"Put it down to my missing you."

She couldn't speak if she'd wanted to. Awake or asleep, she'd thought of him every day since he'd walked out of her life.

"How have you been, Kelly?"

His voice throbbed with tenderness. He gazed at her so tenderly, her heart ached. But she couldn't let him hurt her again.

"Great!" She turned and reached for her gym bag before she could give herself away. "In fact, this afternoon is my last class. I'm packing tonight and leaving in the morning."

"Oh? That's too bad. I had something else in mind for us tonight." Before she could move, he reached behind her neck and undid the ribbon that held back her hair.

"Max…"

He shushed her with a gentle finger on her lips.

"Let me, Kelly. I want to see you the way you were the night at My Blue Heaven. I've never forgotten how beautiful you looked, or how wonderful you felt in my arms. You almost took my breath away."

Desire raced through her. She was filled with a longing to have him hold her in his arms, to kiss her, to ease the yearning in her heart. She took another step backward. Distance was her only defense. What would she do if he took her into his arms?

She was too proud to tell him how hurt she'd been when he'd told her they couldn't fit into each other's lives. She couldn't tell him how unhappy she'd been ever since he left. She only knew she couldn't go through another parting without breaking her heart.

"You should have called before you went to the trouble of coming here," she said. "I would have saved you the trip."

"Where were you planning on going?" His eyes seemed to be focused on her lips. He took another step toward her.

"Los Angeles. I have a job waiting for me there."

To her dismay, Max caught the edge of her towel and slowly, sensuously drew it off her shoulders. Mesmerized by the look in his eyes, she froze.

He touched her bare shoulder with a fingertip and slowly followed the curve of her chin to the right side of her neck where a vein throbbed. "As long as you're looking for a job, would you consider a job in Boston?"

"Boston!" Kelly shivered at the sensuous look that darkened his eyes. "Why would I consider a job in Boston?"

"Because I'm there?"

"That's not a good enough reason for me." She grabbed the towel and wrapped it around her waist. "You once told me I don't fit into your life. And that you didn't think you could fit into mine. I believed you. What's changed?"

He shrugged, but his wry smile lingered. "Me."

Lord help her, that smile and that one-syllable answer was turning her into a mass of quivering jelly. "That's not a good enough reason for me."

"Then how about this?" He took a small jewelry case out of his pocket, snapped open the cover and held it out to her.

The diamonds in the engagement ring nestled in a satin cocoon gleamed under the gym lights. The matching wedding ring was fashioned of entwined slender strands of yellow and white gold. Speechless, she gazed at the rings.

"And this." He took her in his arms and kissed her, so sweetly she thought the gym became bathed in sunshine. His kiss and the taste of his lips were everything she'd longed for and thought never to feel or taste again. The tender pressure of his hands that caressed her back promised more loving to come. She closed her eyes and drank in the scent, the feel of him.

"And this," he said, gently pressing her lips with his own again until she opened to him.

"I love you, Kelly O'Rourke," he whispered. "I hope you love me back. So, tell me. Have you decided if you're ready to be married?"

Now speechless with longing, she struggled for an answer.

The strong beat of his heart, the vein that throbbed

at his throat told her how deeply he felt about her. The longing in his eyes tore at her heartstrings. How could she remind him he'd told her he wasn't ready to marry and have a family? How could she tell him that as soon as he'd left for Boston she'd taken an at-home pregnancy test and that the test results had been positive?

She wanted him so much, she was afraid to ask the questions that tore at her heart and mind. She looked into his eyes, searching for answers to her questions. Was he asking her to marry him because he thought she might be pregnant? Did he want her for herself?

"After you said goodbye, I thought you weren't ever coming back."

He fingered her hair, the nape of her neck. "I came back because I missed you. It got so bad I couldn't work, I was thinking of you all the time." He laughed ruefully. "I even missed that mutt of yours. Where is she?"

"Honey's at home." Kelly had to laugh, too. "The sound of the stereo dance music drives her crazy. She runs around in circles and gets in everyone's way. I had to leave her at home."

"Figures," he answered. "I always said the mutt had a mind of her own." He kissed the tip of her nose, the corners of her eyes, and made his way down to her lips. "Most of all, I came back because I realized Father Joe was right about us—I'd grown to care for you without realizing I'd fallen in love with you. When it dawned on me, I took the first plane out here. And this time, I'm sober and wide-awake."

Kelly caught a glimpse of Damon watching them from the doorway. Behind Max's back, she waved him away. "I have a confession to make, too. I love you back. I'm just not sure I'm ready to be your wife. Not yet. Having you here again is going to take getting used to. Are you willing to wait?"

Max looked disappointed. "Just as long as I don't have to wait any longer than tonight," he answered wistfully. "I had great plans for the two of us, including a visit to that Father Joe of yours. Now, put out your hand."

He took the rings out of the velvet case, reached for her left hand and slipped the rings on her finger. "The engagement ring is a little late, but what the heck. Tradition has its place."

Kelly put her hand over his. "No, please. I'd like to wait for this, too. This time, I want us to be sure there's a future for us."

Max froze, his smile dimmed. "I guess I had that one coming. I thought I had Damon persuaded and that all I had to do is convince your father and Patrick. I never thought I'd have to convince you, too." He took a deep breath. "Do you mind if I give you a kiss to hold us both until you make up your mind?"

Kelly nodded. She wanted more of the kisses she'd been dreaming of since he went away.

When he took her in his arms and kissed her, the gym was transformed into the garish but beautiful honeymoon room at My Blue Heaven. The sound of the gym's air-conditioning unit turned into the strains of beautiful music. The sound of a bugle playing in the dusk became the strains of a welcome-home call for a man she loved with every ounce of her being. She put her heart and soul into the kiss.

"Your kiss isn't exactly a goodbye kiss, sweetheart," Max chided. "Are you sure you don't want to wear the rings?"

"I'm sure." She smiled and touched her lips. "I could get used to these kinds of kisses."

Max put the velvet box back in his pocket. "I'm more than happy to oblige." With a glance to make sure they were alone, he took her in his arms and kissed her again, this time slowly, deeply. When her heart responded, Kelly wanted to believe he was sincere, that he loved her. She may have lingering doubts, but they could wait. There was still the rest of her family to convince.

BY THE TIME they reached the O'Rourke home, her father was waiting for her, Damon at his side. The only one who seemed genuinely pleased to see Max was Honey—until Damon picked her up and deposited her in Kelly's bedroom. Kelly's father didn't look any more accepting of him now than when they met for the first time. Damon glanced at Kelly's still-empty ring finger.

"Damon here tells me you've come back for our Kelly."

Dressed in his uniform, Kelly's father, his mouth set in a straight line, radiated disapproval.

"Yes, sir," Max answered. He was tempted to tell anyone who would listen that "our Kelly" was his Kelly, too. "I found I couldn't keep my mind on business without her."

A new voice sounded. "She's not going anywhere without a marriage certificate!"

Kelly gasped. "I can speak for myself, Patrick O'Rourke!"

"Don't let yourself be swayed by that con artist!" Patrick strode into the room. "I've yet to find any evidence of your wedding license or your marriage certificate." He glared at Max. "Got any answers?"

Max bristled. "I'm tired of having my integrity questioned. I don't have the certificate yet, but if there is one, I intend to find it. But that's another story. I take it you've had me checked out?"

Patrick nodded grimly.

"Find anything?"

"No," Patrick replied, his jaw squared, his eyes cold. "But I have a few questions that need answers."

"You're not the only one," Max said with a glance at Kelly. "Ask away. But by now, it should be pretty obvious to you that I'm not the con man you thought I was."

"I'm not so sure. I still don't understand why there's no record of your marriage to Kelly."

"Give me another week. I'm sure I'll be able to come up with some answers when my cousin gets back from his honeymoon." Max traded stares with Patrick. According to Kelly, her brother's instincts were usually on target. Too bad *he* had to be the guy's target this time. "Or as soon as the assistant manager at the Majestic comes back from his vacation. One way or another, I'm sure one of them has the answer. In the meantime, I intend to remain in Las Vegas."

"A week it is," Kelly's father answered with a stern glance at Max. "And not a day more." Kelly cleared her throat. "That is, if it's all right with my daughter."

Kelly felt four sets of eyes boring into her. Max had asked her if she was ready to be married. In his own way, so had her father. It was time to make up her mind.

From the look on her father's face, it was Max's "one way or another" reply that seemed to bother him. She didn't care. She'd told everyone she was able to make her own decisions. Besides, hadn't she agreed earlier that she and Max were married as long they were on the base? It was now or never.

"I trust Max," she answered. "If he says we're married, then I believe him."

"It's a good thing you feel that way, Kelly. But this time you'd better make sure."

At Damon's remark, everyone's eyes turned on Kelly's brother.

Kelly's Irish temper flared. "And just what do you mean by that remark?"

"Only that Dad could be right. If you're like the rest of the O'Rourkes, there's probably going to be the consequences Dad was talking about."

Chapter Eleven

"Kelly O'Rourke, are you telling me you're expecting?"

Kelly's heart leaped into her throat at her father's roar. Beside her, she heard Max's soft gasp.

This was definitely no way to tell a man he was going to be a father!

As for her own father, in his military uniform, he looked ready for war. "Maybe."

"*Maybe?* If you don't know you're expecting, my girl, who does?"

Max earned her lasting gratitude when he curled his fingers around her hand. "It doesn't matter, sir. If she is, we're very happy about the baby."

Kelly could have kissed Max for intervening before her father really erupted.

"That does it! You and Max are going to be married as soon as possible! Damon, call Father Joe on the telephone and tell him to get the chapel ready. We're coming over!"

"I'm not going anywhere, Dad! I keep telling you I'm already married! Once ought to be enough!"

Her father glowered at her. "You're not married until you get it done right!"

Ignoring the pressure of Max's hand on hers, Kelly glowered back. "I'm not getting married again until I have a chance to meet Max's family!"

Her father's hair seemed to bristle. "And what does that have to do with anything? Max was willing to marry you before he had a chance to meet *your* family, wasn't he?"

"Maybe so," she answered stubbornly. "But I still want to meet them before we make any more plans."

"And what about the story of your wanting to wait here for this cousin of your husband's to come home with some answers? Or for this man from the hotel?" He fixed Max with an accusing stare.

Max shrugged to hide his inner turmoil. The man looked angry enough to shoot him. "Whatever Kelly wants is okay with me."

If Kelly was now back to insisting they were married, why hadn't she accepted the wedding ring?

In the short time he'd known Kelly, he'd already discovered she wasn't the most logical woman on the planet. But, one way or another, she *was* his, and that was all that mattered. Gazing down at her stubborn expression, he got a kick out of the way she stood up to her father.

In the next moment, he realized he was beginning to think like Kelly. The old Max was definitely gone.

"Bah! Young people today," his father-in-law said disgustedly. "Don't you realize that if Father Joe married you, your marriage lines would be more acceptable than a few words shouted over you by someone who didn't even know you?"

Kelly's expression turned ominous. "Acceptable to whom?"

Max squeezed Kelly's hand to warn her to back off before the scene erupted into chaos.

"To me! I'm your father! And for your sainted mother's memory! What would she say about the baby?"

When tears came into Kelly's eyes, Max had had enough. He squeezed her hand again.

"The baby is fine with me, sir. As far as I'm concerned, we Taylors can use some new blood."

Michael O'Rourke sputtered his frustration. Patrick frowned.

Kelly swallowed hard. No matter how confident she'd sounded a few minutes ago, nor how calmly Max was taking Damon's question, she knew in her heart that she *could* be an unwed soon-to-be-mother. And if that wasn't enough to worry about, she'd already blown a treasured O'Rourke tradition to pieces by not marrying in church.

She fought back her tears. "Max, can I see you in my room?"

"Sure, sweetheart." He turned to his audience. "Good night, gentlemen. We'll see you in the morning."

Kelly could hardly wait until the bedroom door closed behind Max. "Do you really feel okay about the baby?"

He eyed her cautiously. "*Is* there a baby?"

She crossed her fingers for good luck. "I think Damon might be right. I could be pregnant."

Max stared at her. Hell, he'd taken Damon's question casually for Kelly's sake, but he hadn't really believed it was true. His legs suddenly felt as if they'd turned to rubber.

If Kelly had broadsided him between the eyes, Max couldn't have felt more stunned. His agenda for his future had already gone to hell in a handbasket, along with his fervent blessings, but he'd never, ever planned on something like this.

"Impossible!" He peered at her middle. "How can you be pregnant?"

"If I have to tell you that—" she started.

Max cut her off. "I didn't mean *that*. I meant we used protection."

Kelly began to see how incongruous the situation was. "Do you remember how once hadn't been enough?"

"Do I ever!" The glaze disappeared from Max's eyes. A sensuous glint replaced it. "What did you mean by you *may* be pregnant? And isn't it too early to tell?"

She felt herself color at the memories that must be going through his mind. "Have you ever heard of at-home pregnancy tests?"

"Of course, but no one I've been around has had a reason to use one." Max's expression changed from incredulous to dazed acceptance in a space of a few seconds, but she could tell his mind was in an uproar. She recognized the feeling—she'd gone through the same sequence of emotions herself a few days ago.

"That's nice to know," Kelly answered with a pleased smile. "Anyway, after I realized a baby could be a possibility, I bought a test. The results were positive. I have an appointment scheduled with my doctor in a week. I'll know for sure after I see him."

Mental images raced through Max's mind with split-second clarity. The morning they'd found themselves in bed together and the discussion of once not having been enough. The conversation on the possibility of babies, and her father's remark about consequences. Now it looked as if they'd finally encountered Consequences—with a capital C.

He felt dazed, yet not exactly worried. Not yet, anyway. A kid was a kid.

At twenty-six, he was probably ready to marry, but he hadn't been in a hurry. Not when the bride chosen for him by their respective parents was more a friend than a lover.

But now there was Kelly. Maybe a wiser force had dealt him a winning hand by connecting him with her. With his and Kelly's respective traditional backgrounds, marriage included babies, didn't it?

On the other hand, it wasn't only the O'Rourke reaction to the baby he was worried about. His own parents were a force to be reckoned with, too. He looked around the room for a place to sit down and chose the nearest surface. The bed.

"When were you going to tell me?" The thought hit him like a Mack truck.

"Not until I was sure about us."

Max sensed a reservation in Kelly's voice. Hadn't she believed him when he'd told her he loved her? Didn't she trust him to make good on his promises? As for a baby, if he was going to be a father, he intended to be her husband, one way or another.

"It's fine with me if I'm going to be a father, but I have to know something, Kelly. Have you made up your mind to trust me to do the right thing by you?"

"I...think so." The hesitancy in her voice gave her away.

Now that he realized his intuition about Kelly's reservations had been right, he was determined to find out what about him was still bothering her. "You're not sure?"

"Maybe. That is, I'm trying to be." Her voice grew more firm, but she still looked uncertain. "I'm more sure when I'm with you."

Max knew from experience that if anyone said "I think so," it meant they *weren't* sure. From the sound of Kelly's voice, she was no different. On the other hand, he'd asked for the truth, hadn't he? He had no one to blame but himself if the truth turned out to be something he didn't want to hear.

He waited until Kelly turned her full gaze on him. "You have to be certain, Kelly. Because after tonight there's no turning back, and not only for the baby's sake."

"I know." Kelly wrapped her arms around herself as if she was cold. She wandered around the room for a few minutes, paused and looked back at him, her eyes still troubled. "I want to believe in happy endings, but—"

Max resisted the urge to grab Kelly, to kiss her and to love her until she believed they could have that happy ending. With all his heart and soul, he wanted to hear her freely say she believed and trusted him without him forcing it out of her. And not only about the status of their marriage, but in *him*.

What would happen if he railroaded her into marriage? What could happen if he turned out to be wrong? He couldn't bear to lose her now.

"Kelly?"

"I wish it could be otherwise. I wish I could be sure there's something more than just a sexual attraction between us."

Max thought of telling her sexual attraction in any relationship was a good place to start. But something about the way Kelly looked at him told him it was no time to be glib.

He tried to put himself in her place, to tell her the words she needed to hear before she gave herself completely.

"Look at it this way, sweetheart. Whatever there is between us has gone beyond sexual attraction, or I wouldn't be here. The facts are that I love you for your spirit, your honesty and the way you're willing to defend me in spite of your doubts. And—" he grinned suggestively "—I'm ready to admit that there *is* that sexual attraction."

Kelly's lips curved in a smile. He was tempted to put an end to the conversation and show her just how he felt about her. Instead, he went on. "If it will give me any points with you, I came back to tell you I'm no longer a programmed robot. Because of you, I've thrown away my agenda. As of now, I'm all yours."

Kelly's eyes lit up with a wicked glint.

Thank God he was getting close.

"So," he said bravely, "is there anything else you want to know?"

"Yes. It's just that I hate to think our relationship started with a one-night stand."

"Agreed. It was, and is, much more than that. But I guess the logical place to start figuring it out is at the beginning—the night we met. Right?"

"Right."

Max took a deep breath. "By now, I think I've figured it all out. My cousin's mind works in obscure ways. Troy has always had a weird sense of humor, especially if it's not at his expense. The way I see it, he and DeeDee must have set us up with the garter ceremony."

Kelly's eyes widened. "You're kidding!"

"No, I'm not. Of course," he added with a smile, "I'll be forever grateful to them if they did. Although, after two days without sleep, I confess I was in no mental state to think clearly that night. Maybe I just got lucky and recognized a good thing when I saw her."

"Do you really think Troy and DeeDee had a hand in it?"

"Can't say for sure," Max answered truthfully. "What I do know is that I fell for you thirty seconds after I took a good look at that enticing leg of yours. And after I looked into your eyes, I was hooked. As for a wedding ceremony, *I* still believe we went through one. And, before this is over, I'm going to not only prove it, I'm going to make you believe it, too. Anything else?"

"There *is* one more thing," Kelly said slowly.

Max's senses jumped to red alert. "I thought so. Might as well get it all out now. I want all your doubts behind you before I show you how much you mean to me. So, what's the problem?"

Kelly studied her hands. "I'm afraid I would only embarrass you if I went home with you. You told me I wouldn't fit into your life in Boston, remember?"

Her distress was so real, Max closed the distance

between them, pulled her into his arms, tipped her face up to his and kissed her nose. "I apologize for the remark. I must have lost my mind. Once my parents meet you and get to know you, I'm sure they'll love you."

Kelly still looked uncertain. "I'm an air force brat and I don't have blue bloodlines. And I'm Irish."

This time Max kissed her tenderly and lovingly. "Don't let that worry you. Like I told your father, the Taylor family could use a little of your kind of bloodlines."

When Kelly closed her eyes and leaned against his chest, Max cursed himself for the misguided bits of information he'd dropped about his family. He remembered telling her that, unlike the O'Rourke clan, his mother and father were straitlaced and dull. But at least one thing they all had in common was a strong belief in traditions.

He stroked Kelly's hair, his mind racing. If she chafed at the O'Rourke hidebound traditions, would she be able to cope with his family's?

"Would we have to live in Boston?"

"I'm afraid so, sweetheart. My business is based there. I can't just walk away from it, at least for now. A lot of people depend on me." He felt her nod against his chest. "Anything else on your list?"

"Yes, one more."

Max held back a groan. "What's that?"

"What about the woman your family expected you to marry? Lian?"

Max was ready with that answer, too. Thank goodness, he could be truthful. "That was before I met you. The fact is, I never took the relationship seriously, or Lian and I would have been married by now. She's a good friend, nothing more. I told her about you before I left. She wished us well.''

Privately, Kelly had her doubts. What woman in her right mind would willingly give up a man like Max?

Torn by indecision, she rested a cheek against his chest and tried to think objectively. In the distance a bugle sounded ''Taps'' as the base flag was being lowered. The base lights came on. She'd lived on military bases all her life and the nightly ritual sounds were comforting. Why had she ever wanted to leave them behind? she wondered. Why had she chafed at the military traditions that had shaped her life, provided her security? Why had she resented the very things her father embraced?

How could she trade her life in the military for life in a big city like Boston?

Before she could wiggle out of Max's arms, Sean barreled into the room. ''Dad told me Max is back!'' He skidded to a stop when he saw her in Max's arms. ''Hey, cool!''

Kelly shrugged and sighed into Max's chest. Her younger brother was irrepressible, but thank heaven, he was harmless.

''Nice to see you, too,'' Max replied. Though the kid's timing was rotten. He recalled how, at fifteen, all he'd thought of were girls and food. Without any of the former, he'd have to bank on the latter's attraction. Now, to get rid of the kid. ''Sean, do you know you're missing dinner?''

Sean regarded him with knowing eyes. The kid was no dummy. He knew when he wasn't wanted. ''Yeah, but first I wanted to see if what Patrick said is true. Are you going to stick around for a while this time?''

''That depends on Kelly.'' His gaze locked with Sean's. Hopefully, the kid would get the message and leave. Then he could go back to convincing Kelly she wanted to be his wife.

''Cool,'' Sean repeated happily. ''I guess I'll go catch up with Dad. You guys want to come along?'' At Max's silence, Sean grinned. ''No, I guess not. See you later.''

Max was about to resume trying to convince Kelly when a scratching sounded behind her bedroom door. ''Too bad your brother couldn't take the mutt with him. It's been one interruption after another since I got here. It looks as if I'm never going to be alone with you.''

Kelly drew away. ''No problem. Once Honey gets a chance to say hello, I'll put her in the kitchen and feed her.''

''It can't be too soon for me,'' Max muttered. ''I might as well get this over with, but give me a minute to brace myself.''

Released from her prison, Honey launched herself at Max. He threw Kelly a what-are-you-going-to-do? look and caught the little dog in his arms. It looked as if her pet had Max converted.

Kelly smiled when Honey quivered with delight and licked Max's face. She smothered a giggle when Max told Honey he was glad to see her, but that enough was enough. He didn't know her pet. Like her owner, enough was never enough.

She teased Honey with a bowl of the dog's favorite puppy food and her favorite toy to send Honey bounding out of Max's arms and into the kitchen. Max brushed dog hairs off himself and sighed with mock relief. "Now, where were we?"

"Boston?"

"Boston? Never heard of the place," Max said solemnly. "But before I show you how much I love you, I'd give a lot to know when you changed your mind about me, sweetheart."

"You're a darn good salesman, Maxwell Taylor. You had me convinced by the time you got around to admitting you first fell in love with my leg before you got around to the rest of me. How many men would confess to something so irrational?"

Irrational? Kelly thought *he* was irrational? The thought was enough to make him laugh. "Does that mean you agree we belong together—no matter what?"

"Yes. But before I make up my mind, I'd still like to check to see if that sexual attraction is still working."

THIS TIME, Kelly's bed looked pleasingly narrow. Instead of worrying about the lack of space, all Max could think of was how conveniently Kelly would fit in his arms. And this time, he vowed as he gazed longingly at her, spoons were out. He wanted her where he could taste her lips, savor her touch and inhale her womanly scent. Tonight, he intended to love her to exhaustion.

"I'll be back in a minute." Kelly gathered up fresh clothing and disappeared into the bathroom.

Max waited impatiently while Kelly showered. He wished he had thought to tell her changing wasn't necessary. That he would have been just as happy to have her dressed in nothing.

He braked his thoughts. Would what he was thinking about doing be good for the baby?

"I love the way you look tonight," he said when she came back into the bedroom dressed in a fresh flannel nightgown, her damp copper hair curling around her shoulders. He sniffed appreciatively. "What's that perfume you're wearing? Something new?"

He could have sworn Kelly blushed.

"Just something I picked up at the Majestic Hotel the other day."

"You went into Las Vegas to buy perfume when there's a perfectly good commissary on the base?"

"It's not exactly perfume, and no one else carries the same brand. I checked. It's called Aromatic Body Butter." She raised an eyebrow. "The label said it has wonderful side effects."

Max took a deeper sniff. He was all for it. As to the advertised side effects, they'd already worked.

"Kelly," he said hesitantly, "what about the baby? Is it going to be okay if we…"

She laughed. "The baby is fifty percent an O'Rourke. We O'Rourkes are up to anything."

He breathed a sigh of relief. If Kelly wanted to re-create the morning after their wedding night, that was okay with him, too.

"Want to try more of those side effects out on me?"

"Yes and no," she answered with a measuring look that sent his senses reeling. "I'm still thinking."

"Then think fast," Max replied. He shucked off

his jacket and shirt. He started on the buckle to his belt before he reconsidered. After talking about an aromatic body butter that was clearly intended to arouse, he was in no condition to be on view. "I'll be in the shower while you do."

Waves of warmth coursed through Kelly at the sensuality behind Max's comment. She wrapped herself in a robe and curled into the rocking chair to think about the future with Max and a baby.

She would tell him she was ready to take up their marriage. That wherever he would go, she'd go, too. Boston was only a question of geography.

As for adapting to his family's different ways, she'd try to make a decent effort. Just as Max was trying to fit into her life, she owed it to him to try to fit into his.

And there would be their baby. Surely having a baby to love would make up for all the differences she might run into.

She was secure in the knowledge that she had truly fallen in love with Max. Confirmed marriage or not, a distant Taylor family or not, it was Max she loved and not any baggage that might come with him. Tonight was the night she would tell him so.

He came back into the bedroom toweling his hair. A dry towel was tied around his waist. She'd caught glimpses of his nude body every time lightning had flashed at the My Blue Heaven Motel, but never as much as this. He was tall, lean and muscular, his shoulders broad, his legs long and firm. And the look in his eyes sent desire shooting through her.

He started to reach for her. "Well, Mrs. Taylor? Have you decided you're ready to be married?"

"Yes."

His hands stopped in midair, then fell to his side at her simple statement. "Do you really mean it this time?"

Kelly nodded.

"Then come over here, sweetheart. I can't take much more of this."

Gazing at Kelly in her quaint nightgown, he began to feel as if tonight was their real wedding night. And the beginning of a real marriage. From the soft, sweet look in her eyes, it was obvious she shared the feeling. He summoned all the love inside him to make this a night they would both remember.

He took a deep breath and caught her hands in his. "I admit you've caught me by surprise, but I'm not sorry about the baby. How about you?"

Kelly shook her head. "No. I've been around baby cousins all my life—all boys. I've always wanted a child of my own. I just hadn't planned on one so soon. But I want to tell you right now, I plan on having a girl."

"Fine with me, as long as she looks like you. We'll even name her Kelly, Jr., if you want."

Kelly's desire for Max was overwhelming. She'd gone through the time he was in Boston afraid she would never feel his arms around her again. Would never know passion in his arms again. The week he'd been away had seemed endless, his return a miracle. This was a moment she'd dreamed of. Tonight, her world was wherever she and Max were together.

Max dropped the towel, threw back the quilt on the bed and held out his arms.

She felt like a bride on her wedding night when

she went into Max's arms. When he folded her into his embrace, she felt that her body fit his as surely as if she were half to his whole. She gazed into eyes shining with tenderness. "I love you, Max," she whispered into his lips. "I'm going to love you forever."

"I love you, too, Kelly," he answered. "As long as we're in this together, everything is going to be okay. Trust me."

Her lips met his with a promise to love, honor, cherish him for all of their days.

"Are you sure it's not the Aromatic Body Butter talking?" he teased when he let her go long enough to catch his breath.

The hot look in his eyes belied his jest. She melted. She loved Max's wry sense of humor almost as much as she loved him. This was a game two could play. "Maybe," she answered doubtfully, "but I'd have to give it a few more tests."

"Test as much as you like," he said as he brushed her hot cheeks with his lips. "But only if you use me as your guinea pig."

His eyes locked with hers. He undid the ribbon ties at her throat and bent to kiss the sensitive spot between her breasts. At his gentle urging, she slid the gown off her shoulders and down to her waist.

"You're so lovely," he said. "I can't get enough of you." He ran his hands over her skin, slowly drew off her nightgown and let it drop to the floor. He rained kisses over her neck, her shoulders, her breasts and where his child nestled. She heard him murmur, "With a bride like you, who needs Aromatic Body Butter?"

Chapter Twelve

Three days later, Max pulled up in front of a classic redbrick house in the Back Bay district of Boston. "Look, sweetheart. We're home."

Kelly looked. The four-story town house was a picture out of a history book. At least one hundred years old, it spoke of old wealth and blue bloodlines. Gleaming cut-glass windowpanes fronted the street. A black iron knocker in the shape of an anvil was set into an artistically carved white front door. The ornamental black iron fence protected the house from the street. The building spelled anything but "home" to her.

The contrast between the formal town house and the series of government-provided housing she'd lived in all her life was intimidating. She stirred uncomfortably as the contrast sank in. "How long are we going to stay here?"

Max swung around to look at her. His smile faded. "I thought you'd be pleased."

"The house is beautiful, but it belongs to your parents," she answered honestly. "I was hoping for a home of our own."

"If that's all that's worrying you, you can relax. The top floor was turned into a bachelor's apartment for me some years back."

When she didn't look convinced, Max apologized. "Sorry, Kelly, I guess I wasn't thinking. If you'd rather, we can check into a hotel until we find a place of our own."

Kelly shook her head. Max had gone along with her, she owed him. "I promised myself I'd try to adapt to your life. I just didn't fully realize the extent to which your family came along with it." She bit her lower lip and gazed at the house again. The differences between her military-style way of life and Max's loomed larger than ever. "I intend to keep that promise."

"You're sure, Kelly? I don't want you to do anything that will make you unhappy."

She took a deep breath and tried to smile. She was used to wide-open spaces with plenty of room to breathe, where children could play. The Taylor town house had no open grounds. And even more disturbing, it fronted on a major street. It was definitely not the place to bring up a small child. But if this was what Max wanted, she had to compromise.

"Yes, I'm sure. It was just a passing reaction. Your apartment will be fine. At least, until the baby is born."

Max hugged her. "That's my girl."

Kelly bristled silently, just as she had whenever someone called her a girl. The military had been an all-male institution, at least until recently. She'd been dominated by strong men for so long, she'd looked forward to being on her own. Or, at least, married to a man who treated her as an equal.

Why couldn't Max accept she was a grown woman, soon to be a mother? Why couldn't he understand that she wanted to create a home where her children could grow up and run free, just as she and her brothers had done? A fourth-floor apartment in a town house wasn't her idea of the place to begin.

Max eyed her warily. "Maybe you'll feel better once we're inside. I'll have someone drive the car out back and unload our things." He came around the car and opened the door for her. "Come with me, sweetheart. Everything is going to be okay, you'll see. I have my own key," he explained under his breath as he used the iron knocker. "It's just that my mother hates surprises."

Kelly was tempted to hold back. What kind of family life did Max have, she wondered, if someone had to let him into his own parents' house? And if Max had told his mother he was coming home and bringing a wife with him, why would she be surprised?

"Max, wait a minute!" She caught his arm before he could knock again. "You *did* tell your parents you were bringing me home with you, didn't you?"

"Yes. Dad's away on a business trip, but I told my mother. Why?"

"Why?" Kelly echoed. The chagrined look on his face gave him away. There was more behind his simple yes than he was willing to admit. "Is there something I ought to know before we go in?"

He lifted the door knocker again. "Not to worry. It's just that I didn't give my mother all the details about us, but I'm sure—"

The front door was flung open before he could explain what details he'd omitted. "Maxwell! Welcome home!" A smiling older woman in an immaculate black skirt and white blouse stood in the door beaming at Max. She smelled of sugar and spice and chocolate chips. All the homey, domestic scents Kelly associated with her own mother.

Her mother-in-law?

Max went into the woman's open arms. "Hi, Nancy, it's good to be home." He reached back for Kelly's hand and drew her close. "Nancy, this is my wife, Kelly. Kelly, this is Nancy Carter, our housekeeper. Nancy's been with the family since I was a kid."

"Welcome, Mrs. Taylor." The housekeeper smiled her pleasure and held open the door. "When Maxwell called to say he was married and bringing home a wife, I thought he was talking about someone else."

Kelly grew uneasy. Not only was Nancy *not* her mother-in-law, she had clearly expected Max to bring home a different bride. Was her identity one of the details Max had forgotten to tell his family?

"Do come in, Mrs. Taylor," the housekeeper went on. "It's about time this young man found himself a wife. If there's anything I can do for you, just let me know." She raised an eyebrow in a silent message to Max. "Your mother is upstairs. I expect she'll be down as soon as she hears your voice."

Before Kelly could return the housekeeper's greeting, a teenage girl rushed into the hall and threw herself into his arms. "Thank goodness you're home, Max! It's so lonely here when you're not home. Please tell me you're going to stay!"

Laughing, he held her at arm's length. "I will if you let me up for air. I brought someone with me." He reached back for Kelly's hand and pulled her to him. "Say hello to my wife, Kelly. Kelly, this is my sister, Jeane. She's home from school on some holiday or other."

"Hi, Kelly." Jeane grinned. "I'm home for Easter break, but it's been awful here without someone to talk to. Mom doesn't count," she added in a whisper. "When I heard Max got married, I thought his wife was— Oh, never mind about that." She hugged Kelly. "Am I ever glad to see you!"

Intrigued, Kelly hugged her back. Jeane reminded her of Sean—outspoken and cheerful—and usually in trouble. She put her questions about the "someone else" the housekeeper had mentioned behind her. "I'm very happy to meet you, too."

"Cool!" Jeane glanced over her shoulder. "Now that Max is married, maybe there'll be some life in this dull old place."

"Jeane! That will be enough!"

Kelly's heart skipped a beat. The woman who glided down the stairs was tall and patrician. A single strand of pearls hung around the neck of her black woolen dress, matching pearl studs were in her ears. Not a strand of her blond hair was out of place.

Jeane winked at Kelly. "Yes, Mother."

The elegant newcomer turned her gaze on Kelly and Max. "Maxwell?"

"Hello, Mother." He put his arm around Kelly's shoulder as if to protect her. If he meant to reassure her, the pressure of his arm didn't cut it. "Mother, this is Kelly O'Rourke. My wife."

His mother smiled at Kelly with patent falseness. "How do you do?"

Kelly swallowed a reply as she compared the woman's aloof greeting with the hearty Irish welcome Max had received from her own family. And the hilarity with which he'd been accepted into the O'Rourke clan. The housekeeper's welcome had been warmer than this. Undaunted, Kelly returned her mother-in-law's enigmatic gaze with a studied smile of her own.

"Do come inside the parlor, Maxwell, Kelly. You must be exhausted from your flight. Nancy," Max's mother called over her shoulder, "please bring tea."

"Don't let Mother scare you off," Jeane muttered behind Kelly's back. "She's really harmless. It'll take a while, but you'll get used to her. Whoops, I'm not supposed to say things like that, huh, Max?"

"Not if you want to stay out of trouble," Max answered under his breath.

Somehow, Kelly didn't feel reassured at the banter. Nor did she look forward to waiting to feel at home.

Andrea Taylor turned her gaze on Max. "I don't mind telling you this is unexpected."

Kelly was dismayed. Where was a mother's welcome at meeting her son's wife for the first time?

Max frowned. "I wouldn't call it unexpected. I told you a week ago I'd gotten married."

"Yes, indeed." His mother's gaze turned on Kelly. "What you neglected to tell me was the name of the bride."

"That's only because I wanted to surprise you."

"You know I don't care for surprises," his mother answered with a frown. "Now, where were we?" She turned back to Kelly. "Max told me the two of you were married in Las Vegas?" Kelly nodded. "If we'd known what Max intended, his father and I would certainly have arranged to be there. Frankly," she added with a sharp glance at Max, "I don't understand why we weren't invited to the wedding."

"That's because it was a spur-of-the-moment elopement." Max put his arm around Kelly's shoulder. "Right, Kelly?"

"A spur-of-the-moment elopement?" Andrea frowned. "I've heard there are all kinds of ways to get a marriage license at any time of the day or night in Las Vegas. I hope it's legal."

Max glanced at Kelly. "I'm sure it was."

His mother turned her gaze on Kelly. "Are you sure you're married?"

Before Kelly could answer, Max jumped in. "We're sure, Mother. As for marrying so suddenly, I couldn't help myself. It was love at first sight—that is," Max added with a self-conscious laugh, "after I caught the garter."

His mother's eyebrows rose an inch. "Garter?"

Kelly smothered a groan. Max's mother didn't look too happy, either. If Max had intended to call off his mother's suspicions he'd made a big mistake.

Jeane choked on her laughter.

"The *bride's* garter, Mother," Max hurriedly added. "I caught the garter and was sliding it up Kelly's leg when—"

"That's enough," his mother interjected with a wave of her hand. "I don't think I care to hear any more."

"Come on, Mother," Max teased. "There's probably a picture in your wedding album where some-one's pointing to a garter on your leg.''

His mother bridled. "I would never allow such a thing, Maxwell! And if you were a gentleman, you wouldn't mention it. Let alone marry a woman you didn't know!"

Kelly was ready to take her on when the house-keeper came into the room. She carried an elaborate silver tea service and placed the tray in front of Max's mother. "I brought some of Max's favorite cookies," she said with a smile as she winked at Kelly.

"I must say, Maxwell," his mother remarked as she poured tea, "your father and I expected more of you than this."

"I don't see why. You and Dad have been after me for some time to get married and start a family."

"Perhaps, but we certainly didn't expect this," his mother answered with a glance at Kelly.

For Kelly, her mother-in-law's message was clear. Max's parents had expected him to marry and start a family—but not with her as his wife. Lian?

"And why not?" Max demanded. "The choice of a wife was mine. I chose Kelly."

Kelly realized Max was having difficulty under-standing where his mother was coming from. She cleared her throat. "Max, please..."

"No, Kelly. I'm entitled to an answer. Mother?"

"Quite simply, we thought you had other plans. We all believed it was Lian you were going to marry."

"Lian is a good friend, but that's all," Max replied grimly. "In fact, before I went back to Las Vegas, I had a long talk with her. She understood."

"Understood? How could she have understood practically being left at the altar. After all, we had the two of you paired off for a long time."

"*You* had us paired off. *I* didn't. I've apologized to Lian for not telling her long ago that I thought of her as a good friend, but that was all. I also told her that from the moment I looked into Kelly's eyes, I knew she was mine. In fact, I consider myself a lucky man."

Kelly's heart was full to overflowing at Max's open declaration of love. She knew how hard it was to stand up to one's parents, and the guilty feeling that lingered.

"I feel lucky too, Mrs. Taylor," she added quietly. "Max and I love each other very much."

"So I see," his mother agreed with a measuring look at Kelly. She poured a cup of tea and handed it to Kelly. "Tell me, is your home in Las Vegas?"

"Thank you," Kelly murmured. "For the present. Actually, I've lived in a number of places around the world."

Andrea Taylor arched an eyebrow. "For the present?"

Kelly sipped the hot tea to calm her rebellious stomach. "My father's in the air force. We moved whenever he was reassigned."

"My goodness!" Mrs. Taylor paused in the middle of pouring Max tea. "How does your mother feel about that?"

"We lost her some time ago. But I never heard her complain." Kelly couldn't help comparing Max's distant mother to her own late loving mother. Ice and fire. Indifference and love. No wonder Max was so taken by the warmth of the gregarious and friendly O'Rourkes.

She glanced around the room that, according to Max, had been home to generations of Taylors. High ceilings with crown moldings, priceless antique furniture, valuable landscapes on the walls. All beautiful, but nothing compared to the simple personal items and family pictures her mother had lovingly cherished through the years.

"How unfortunate for you, my dear. It's so important to have a stable environment. And the rest of your family?"

Kelly wanted to tell her a loving environment was more important than a stable, if distant, one. Instead, she described her three brothers.

"A policeman?" Her mother-in-law looked shocked.

From the expression on her mother-in-law's face, Kelly fully expected to be told a Taylor ancestor had signed the Declaration of Independence. "Yes, and proud of it," Kelly replied, fighting to keep her temper. "My older brother Damon is a career air force officer. We're proud of him, too. My younger brother, Sean, is still in school."

Andrea set her teacup on the table. "How interesting. Now, tell me how you and Max met and married so precipitously."

"Let me tell the story, sweetheart." Max intervened. "That is, if you're sure I won't offend you again, Mother."

"That depends. Go ahead."

Kelly was grateful she didn't have to explain how she'd awakened to find Max in bed with her. She was in the mood to tell it straight, but realized it was the last thing to do if she was going to reside in the same house as Max's parents.

"To start with," Max began, "you remember I went to Las Vegas to attend Troy and DeeDee's wedding?" His mother nodded. "Well, Kelly was DeeDee's maid of honor. During the festivities, Troy threw the garter to a bunch of us bachelors." He stopped to grin at Kelly. "I was the lucky guy who caught it."

"Wow!" Jeane sat on the edge of her chair. "Go on. What happened next?"

"The next thing I knew, I was asked to put the garter on the maid of honor's leg. That's when I really noticed Kelly."

His mother gasped her disapproval. "Do you mean to say you'd never met Kelly before then?"

Max's face was a picture of chagrin. He back-tracked hurriedly. "No, I meant it was the first time I *really* noticed her. Before the night was over, I proposed to Kelly and she accepted."

"My goodness!" His mother dabbed at her lips with a pristine linen napkin. "Tell me, did the two of you give any thought to the future before you rushed to get married?"

Max frowned. "How do you mean?"

"It's your duty to carry on the Taylor name. Your children will be carrying on the Taylor name, or have you forgotten?"

Kelly gasped at the implication that her children might not meet Taylor-family standards.

"Mother," Max warned with an apologetic glance at Kelly. "It's premature to talk about children. Kelly and I have been married for less than a month. I don't think this is the time or place to discuss children.''

Andrea pursed her lips. ''Nevertheless, children *are* a natural consequence of marriage.''

Kelly shuddered. Children a consequence? With an attitude like that, no wonder Max and his sister grew up in boarding schools. And no wonder Max was only just beginning to think for himself, to live without a predetermined agenda.

Max rose and pulled Kelly to her feet. ''You may be disappointed by my choice, but Kelly is special and I love her. We're still on our honeymoon and I won't allow you to spoil it.''

''Nevertheless, it's time to consider the consequences, Maxwell.'' His mother rose to her feet. ''I'm sure it's been a long day for both of you. We can talk about this later. It's too bad your father's not home.''

''You're right, Mother. It *has* been a long day. Come on, Kelly, I'll take you upstairs.''

''You will come down for dinner, won't you?''

''Kelly?'' Max looked at her for the answer. This was their first night home, and if that stricken look didn't leave Kelly's face, he was determined it would be his last.

Kelly nodded. ''Yes, of course.''

Andrea Taylor smoothed nonexistent creases from her dress. She glanced at her watch. ''I'll tell Nancy to set places for you. I'll expect you at eight.''

Max led Kelly to a door in the hall. ''Luckily, my grandparents put in an elevator some years back.''

''Good,'' she murmured, glancing at the curving staircase. ''I was afraid we'd have to climb up three stories. The way I feel, I'm not sure I'm up to it.''

"Not to worry," Max said sympathetically as he opened the door to the elevator. "The floor below this one actually is the first floor. That makes my apartment only two flights up. But we can use the elevator anytime."

Uneasy with Max's explanation, Kelly contemplated the proximity of the elevator to the parlor. "Will we have to come through here every time we go out?"

"No. It's just easier because of the elevator. If you'd rather, there's the kitchen stairs around the back with a separate entrance for a quick getaway. I use them all the time."

Kelly tried to smile at Max's attempt at humor. "If I wasn't so tired, that might be funny."

Max sobered. "It's more than the stairs that's bothering you, isn't it? Is it because the family lives so close?"

"That's part of it," she answered honestly. "But I suppose I can use the back stairs."

"And is what my mother said bothering you, too?"

"Yes, I'm afraid so." Kelly looked up at him with tears in her eyes. "Oh, Max, your mother doesn't seem too happy about your marrying me. Maybe we ought to tell her the truth—that we're not sure we really *are* married."

"The truth is that I love you and that if we're not already married, we're going to be. So don't let my mother get to you." He grazed her wan cheek with a fingertip. "She means well. It's just that she's always prided herself on our family history."

Kelly exploded. "And what makes you think the O'Rourkes don't? And that includes Uncle Jake and my aunt Brigid, but you didn't hear *them* talking that way. O'Rourkes may not have come over with the *Mayflower,* but we have a history, too!'' She paused for breath. ''And I don't like being patronized!''

''Kelly O'Rourke Taylor, do you realize we're having our first real marital argument?''

''Can I get in on it, too?'' Jeane sailed into view. ''I just told Mother she was too hard on you. She's banished me for being too outspoken.''

''That's nothing new.'' Max laughed, grateful for the break in tension between himself and Kelly. ''What did you say now?''

''I told her we ought to be grateful to Kelly for bringing fresh blood into the family.''

Max didn't have the heart to ask Jeane to leave, not when she looked so proud of herself. She was right on target. The Taylor bloodlines were too blue and too thin. The family needed someone like Kelly to warm them up. Given the chance, Kelly was just the one to do it.

''I'll see you later, sis.'' Max opened the door to the elevator. ''We're going upstairs so Kelly can get some rest. If I were you, I'd get out of sight until Mother calms down.''

''Okay,'' Jeane sighed. ''I was hoping to hear more about the way you and Kelly married.''

''No way.'' Max laughed again. ''The rest of the story is Kelly's and my secret, right, sweetheart?'' At Kelly's smile he said, ''Come on, the elevator is at your service.''

''The apartment is actually a four-room suite,'' he explained as they rode up. See, there's a living room, kitchen, two bedrooms and a bath. Once you get used to it, I'm sure you'll like the arrangement.''

Kelly's heart sank. The only arrangement she wished for was a home of her own. The small rooms ahead were to the right of a long, narrow hall. The living room was decorated in brown and burgundy with cherry-wood furniture—a man's room. She felt the walls were closing in on her.

She shut her eyes and fought for self-control. How could she live here, let alone raise a child in such a sterile environment? And how would Honey fit in when she sent for her?

''Like it?''

Kelly fought off a growing feeling of nausea. ''I think I'd better lie down.'' She swayed as she spoke.

''Kelly!'' Max grabbed her before she fell. ''Are you all right?''

''I will be as soon as I rest a while. Maybe it's morning sickness, or maybe I'm claustrophobic from the narrow hallway. I'm sure I'll feel better as soon as the nausea passes.''

''I hope so,'' Max muttered. ''Otherwise dinner is going to be an eye-opener.''

''Why? Are you afraid your mother will find out I'm pregnant?''

''No, of course not,'' Max answered hurriedly. ''I'm sorry. I was just thinking out loud.'' He led the way down the hall to a bedroom. He pointed to a pair of windows. ''If knowing makes you feel better, there's a fire escape out there. My mother protested it ruined the architectural value of the house, but the fire department insisted.''

Kelly looked out the window to the backs of a row

of town houses across a small service yard. Used to the large backyards at home, she shuddered. "Thank God," Kelly murmured. "Otherwise the place could be a firetrap."

"That's what the fire inspector told my mother." He laughed. "She threatened to withdraw her support of the Fireman's Fund, but she lost the argument. She usually wins."

"Until I came along," Kelly added ruefully.

"Come on, Kelly, I'm sure the two of you are going to become friends. Give it some time."

For Max's sake, Kelly agreed.

She gazed at the king-size bed, dresser, table and lamps and a small desk. Their luggage was set in a corner. A fire was burning in the fireplace.

She focused on the king-size bed. It would never mean as much to her as her narrow bed back home in Las Vegas. A bed where she and Max had shared their thoughts and had gotten to know each other. Where he'd curled himself around her, held her close and given her pleasure beyond her dreams. Even the double bed in the My Blue Heaven Motel had more meaning.

"I think I'll just sit here for a while," she said, dropping into a large leather chair in front of the fire. She warmed her hands, but the cold ache in her heart remained.

Max hovered over her. "Are you sure there's nothing I can do for you, sweetheart?"

"Hot tea and some crackers might help."

"Right away." He picked up the telephone. "Nancy, could you please send up some hot tea and crackers in the dumb waiter?

Kelly protested. "Max! Now Nancy will think I'm pregnant. I noticed a kitchen when we came in. Why can't we make our own tea?"

"Sorry." He grinned sheepishly. "I travel a lot and I hardly ever use the kitchen. I might have tea somewhere, but I'm sure I don't have crackers around. Anyway, Nancy's always downstairs willing to play mother."

Kelly despaired of making Max understand she wanted to make the apartment a home for them. And if Nancy Carter played mother, it was because Max's own mother didn't fill the role. She moaned under her breath. What kind of life had she committed herself to?

She felt too drowsy to argue. She leaned back in the large chair and closed her eyes. She was no cook but she planned to learn how to cook Max's favorite foods. No way did she intend to eat downstairs with Max's mother and father, or have Nancy do the cooking.

The tinkle of bells startled her.

Kelly opened her eyes to see Max leaning over her. "Nancy sent up a tray for you." He offered her a cup of hot tea. "It looks as if she's under the impression you have a cold. See, you didn't have to worry after all."

Kelly sipped the tea and nibbled at a cracker. The way her stomach was churning, it was all she could do to keep both down. "Maybe I ought to take a nap."

Max helped her out of the chair. "Sure. I have a few telephone calls to make, anyway. I'll turn down the bed for you and wake you up in time to go down for dinner.''

Kelly fell asleep but her dreams of a carefree family dinner were shattered by the vision of Max's mother.

MAX TOOK the opportunity to call his cousin while Kelly rested. "Troy! Thank God you're home. I was afraid I wasn't going to be able to reach you in time.''

"Hi, Max. Even honeymoons have to end. So, how are things— Hey, what was that you said? In time for what?''

Max took a deep breath, looked over his shoulder at the door behind him and lowered his voice. "I'm not doing too well here. In fact, I'm in trouble.''

"Trouble?'' Troy's laugh came through the phone. "What kind of trouble could you have gotten into?''

"It's about Kelly. Kelly O'Rourke.''

Troy laughed again. "The last time I saw you, you and Kelly were having a wonderful time.''

"More than you know. In fact, I woke up the next morning and found myself in bed with her.''

"Hey, cousin,'' Troy chided, "that's a bit much for a square guy like you, isn't it?''

"That's not all. In fact, I think Kelly and I got married!''

"Give me a minute to digest that,'' Troy replied after a silence. "DeeDee wanted the two of you to get together, but I didn't know you cared enough for Kelly to marry her.''

Max sighed. "It was easy. I fell in love. In fact, I was hooked after I looked into her eyes.''

"Wow! You mean you fell in love with Kelly because of her eyes?"

"That," Max agreed, thinking of Kelly's lithe leg, killer smile and satin skin, "and a few other little things."

"Other things?"

Max wasn't about to share *all* the things about Kelly that had attracted him. His thoughts were too personal, too full of sensual memories, and he was too anxious to settle the question of what had happened the night of Troy's wedding. "Anyway, the reason for my call is to ask you if you remembered how Kelly and I happened to get married."

"Good God! Get real. How would I remember something like that if you can't remember it?"

"Something happened," Max insisted. "And knowing you the way I do, you had to have been in on it."

"Well, to tell the truth, I remember that things did get a little complicated there when the TV and newspaper media burst into the chapel. I'm just not sure about what happened."

"Come on, Troy, I was counting on you. If you don't remember, I guess I'll have to go back to Las Vegas and follow up with Bennett when he's back and look for a marriage license or a wedding certificate."

"Who's Bennett?"

"The assistant manager of the Majestic. He congratulated me on my marriage the next morning. He *must* know something. There's a lot riding on his answer."

"Wait a minute! You're not saying that Kelly is—"

"Yes. It looks as if Kelly is expecting. And without a legal father..." Max's voice died away. "That's why a marriage license or wedding certificate is so important—for the kid's sake. In fact, the way things are going, I'm not sure it wasn't all a dream."

Kelly awakened at the sound of Max's voice. Her sleep had been troubled, filled with visions of Max's mother shaking an accusing finger. She stirred uncomfortably in the king-size bed that was too big, too soft, too lonely without Max. She rose, put on a robe and made her way to the small living room.

She froze outside the door in time to hear Max say he wasn't sure they were married. Or that there *was* a marriage license! He'd been assuring her for weeks that he recalled their being married the night they met. Now he wasn't sure?

It wasn't that revelation that got to her—she'd known about the elusive marriage certificate from the beginning. It was the way Max talked about the baby that bothered her. Almost as if it was his duty to the baby to have come back for her. And the reason why he was sticking with her.

"Max!"

Max looked over his shoulder. "Sorry, Troy. I have to go now. I'll talk to you later." He hung up the phone.

"Feeling better, sweetheart?"

"No! But that's beside the point. I thought you swore you recalled our being married."

"I do."

"That's not what I heard you tell your cousin."

"Now wait a minute, Kelly. I thought you were sleeping. If you'd arrived earlier, you would have heard me tell Troy I loved you. That I fell in love with you the first time I looked into your eyes."

"Love! I've heard that line before," Kelly scoffed. "The point is, you lied to me. From what I heard you tell Troy, you aren't too happy about the baby."

"Kelly, sweetheart, you're mistaken," Max pleaded. "You're tired and you're not feeling well. Why don't you go back and lie down until you feel better. We can talk about this after dinner."

"No," Kelly said firmly. "We'll talk about it now. I thought you came back for me because you loved me, believed I *was* your wife. I wanted to believe you loved me as much as I loved you. And that you wanted this baby as much as I do."

"Kelly," he pleaded, "what's come over you? You said you believed me before."

"That's because I wanted to believe you. Now I think you came back for me only to find out if I was pregnant. And that when you found out I was, you stayed. Maybe it was because you thought that the Taylor family's honor was at stake."

"Come on, Kelly, you're wrong. I love you and I want to be your husband. Why won't you believe me?"

"I can't." She turned back to the bedroom. "Tell your mother I'm too tired to come down for dinner. In the morning, I'm going home where I belong."

Chapter Thirteen

In the end, he had to let Kelly go. He had to let her go because he loved her.

A plane sped down the runway, roared into the sky and turned west in a graceful arc as Max drove out of the airport. From its familiar markings, it was the plane carrying Kelly home and taking his heart with her.

Nothing he'd said earlier had moved her. Not his apology for his mother's behavior, nor his insistence he'd come back to Las Vegas for Kelly for her own sake. What had seemed to disturb Kelly most of all was her renewed belief he wouldn't have wanted her if he hadn't thought she might be pregnant.

Nothing he'd said had convinced her he loved her for herself. Not even when he told her he'd somehow known they belonged together from the moment he'd held her in his arms while dancing after the garter ceremony. The romantic music, the way her body fit to his, the challenging and sexy gleam in her eyes— they had combined to seduce him. He wasn't actually sure who had seduced whom, but the end results had been fantastic.

It was after that that the night had evaporated in a romantic haze.

He'd tried to tell her he was positive he'd heard someone pronounce them husband and wife. Granted, the rest of the night might have been fuzzy, but he was damn sure about the marriage part.

Through no fault of his own, events had prevented him from finding the proof he needed. He vowed to find it soon or his name wasn't Maxwell Taylor.

By the time he pulled up at the Taylor town house, his mind was made up. He was going to Las Vegas on the next available flight and claim his wife. And this time, he vowed, he wasn't going to give up until he found the proof he needed to convince everyone of the facts. If he couldn't find proof—an unbearable thought—he was determined to woo Kelly and marry her in front of every O'Rourke able to walk, drive or fly to the ceremony.

To avoid a scene, he took the back stairs to his apartment.

"Maxwell?" his mother sailed into his bedroom. A frown creased her forehead. "Where's Kelly?"

"On her way home," he answered briefly. He dropped his suitcase on the bed and, for the first time in his life, wanted to sound off to his mother. But she *was* his mother and he owed her respect. "Next time, Mother, please knock before you come in."

"Maxwell!" His mother dropped onto the bed and clutched her heart. "You've changed since you married Kelly. I hardly know you."

"It's me, all right." Max gazed at her for a long moment before he shook his head. "The problem is that you don't seem to realize I'm a married man.

You keep treating me as if I'm still a child in your home. Big mistake. Bringing Kelly here opened my eyes. This is your home, not mine,'' he added painfully. ''After you got through with her, Kelly felt she didn't belong here.''

''Not your home? Of course it's your home. You're a Taylor,'' she said as if that settled the issue. ''As for Kelly leaving, I hope it wasn't something I said.''

''Yes. Actually, it was.'' Frustrated by his mother's inability to understand the situation, he went on frankly. ''You should have realized how you would sound to Kelly before you made your remarks about our children. You didn't make an effort to make her feel welcome.''

''I only intended to point out the differences between the two of you. After all, they *are* important—especially when it comes to children.''

''Important to you, but not to me,'' Max answered bitterly. ''The O'Rourkes are fine people. And, let me tell you, they were a heck of a lot nicer to me than you were to Kelly.'' He added shirts and ties to the slacks he'd already packed in the suitcase.

His mother had the grace to look embarrassed. ''I'm sorry, really I am. I never meant to hurt Kelly. What are you going to do now?''

''I'm out of here. I'm going to Las Vegas to take care of a few things.''

''What things?''

Max snapped the suitcase shut and shrugged into a jacket. ''Brace yourself, Mother. You're going to have the heir you wanted. You may not like the idea, but Kelly's the mother and you're going to become a grandmother.''

His mother gasped. "A grandmother? So soon? Are you saying you married Kelly because she's pregnant?"

"No. I married her because I love her," he answered with a growing sense of satisfaction. He hefted the suitcase. "And before you say something you might regret later, let me tell you the kid will be as much an O'Rourke as a Taylor."

His mother sank back on the bed, her face softening in an anxious smile. "You *are* coming back, aren't you?"

Max paused. "For a visit, maybe. When I get through convincing Kelly we belong together, I intend to set up a home of my own. Wherever Kelly wants."

"Oh, Maxwell, dear. I don't know what to say."

"Don't say anything," Max cautioned. "I hate to leave you this way, Mother, but I'm going after the woman I love. And it doesn't mean that I don't love you. Why don't you use the next few months to get used to the idea of being a grandmother?"

THE MAJESTIC WAS CROWDED with tourists admiring the eye-catching decor. Would-be guests were lined up three deep in front of the check-in counter. In the discreet distance, the clinking sounds of slot machines could be heard.

This was the place where people came in the hopes of making their dreams come true. It was the place where he and Kelly had met. The first thing on his agenda was to find out if this was the place where they'd gotten married.

He signed the registration form at the hotel desk. "I'd like to speak to Reggie Bennett, please."

The clerk stopped in mid-welcoming smile. "Is there something wrong? Mr...." He glanced down at Max's signature, "Mr. Taylor?"

"No, not yet," Max answered grimly. "You might call Bennett and tell him I'm on my way to his office. In the meantime, please have someone take my bag up to my room."

"Of course, Mr. Taylor. I'll call Mr. Bennett right away."

When Max reached the hotel's business office, Reggie Bennett came out to greet him.

"Hello, again." Bennett beamed. He looked over Max's shoulder. "And where's the new Mrs. Taylor?"

"That's what I came here to see you about," Max replied. "Where can we go to talk privately?"

"Come on inside." Bennett glanced at his watch. "Janet just left for the day so you'll have your privacy. What's on your mind?"

Max followed him inside and closed the door behind him. "You once congratulated me on getting married at the hotel. Right?"

"Right." Bennett's expression turned anxious. "You're not here for a divorce, are you?"

"God, no," Max answered. "But I do have a problem. I haven't been able to locate my marriage certificate. Do you happen to have it?"

Bennett frowned. "You lost me. Why would I have your marriage certificate? You're the one who got married."

Max blew. "Because *I* don't! And neither does anyone else I've asked."

"I don't get it." Bennett thought for a moment.

"Assuming you gave your wedding license to the minister, he would have been the one to fill out the certificate and sign it. If he didn't give it to you that night, he must have mailed it. Why don't you ask him?"

"I would have," Max answered wryly, "provided I'd applied for a marriage license in the first place." Disheartened, he dropped into the chair in front of Bennett's desk.

"You *did* apply for a license, didn't you?"

"Not according to Janet's cousin Flora. The one who works at the marriage bureau."

"Sounds as if you do have a problem. You do realize, don't you, that without a license, you might not be married after all?"

"I don't have to be a genius to figure that one out. What I want to know is, why did you congratulate me on my marriage the following morning when you delivered the complimentary wedding breakfast?"

"Probably for the same reason you thought you were married. I'd seen and heard the minister pronounce you husband and wife the night before. That's why I authorized the desk clerk to give you and Mrs. Taylor the bridal suite instead of the single room you got when you registered." A thought occurred to him. "Say, you're not going to sue the hotel, are you?"

Max leaned forward. At last! Marriage license or not, this was the first real affirmation he and Kelly *had* been married! "Are you sure about the minister?"

"Sure. In fact— Wait a minute." Bennett reached for a folder he kept on a table behind him. "You and Mrs. Taylor were the one thousandth couple to get married in our new wedding chapel—that was the reason for the big celebration. In fact, I have photographs of your final vows right here.'' He grinned as he held out the photographs. ''Don't see how I could have made a mistake. Do you?''

''You don't know the half of it,'' Max muttered as he studied the photographs. ''I hope this isn't a case of not being able to believe everything you see.'' He sank back in his chair. ''The truth is, my cousin Troy Taylor and his wife were the bride and groom. Kelly was the maid of honor and I was the best man.''

''You don't say! What happens now?''

Max sighed. ''I think it's a case of starting at the beginning and then seeing my wife about living happily ever after. Without some explanation, I don't have a prayer of getting her back.'' He rose and held out his hand. ''Thanks for your help. I may have to get back to you later, okay?''

''Sure. I'll think good thoughts on your behalf,'' Bennett agreed. He shook Max's hand and slapped him on the back. ''It looks as if you're going to need all the help you can get.''

''Amen,'' Max muttered. He headed for his room, some strong coffee and a telephone. His reunion with Kelly would have to wait.

The beginning was obviously Troy and DeeDee's wedding. From there, he intended to hand Kelly proof they were actually married. *If* there was any proof to be had.

He didn't intend to stop there, either. One way or another he planned to convince Kelly they belonged together and to get married again.

He ordered room service and settled down to some

detective work. First on the list was to call his cousin at home in Los Angeles. To his relief, Troy was at home.

"Troy? Max. I have to talk to you."

"Sure, pal. Wait a minute while I turn down the television. What's up?"

"Before we start, is DeeDee around?"

"No, she's gone next door for a few minutes. Why?"

"Because I don't want her to hear what I have to ask you."

There was a cautious silence at the other end of the line. "Are you still in some kind of trouble?"

"Yeah," Max answered wearily. He pushed the untouched room-service cart away. The way he felt, he might never eat again. At least, not until he had Kelly back. "By the way, I forgot to ask you if you enjoyed your honeymoon."

"It was great," Troy answered cheerfully. "I heartily recommend married life. How about you?"

"That's the problem. I couldn't tell you the whole story yesterday because Kelly came in and interrupted me. Bottom line, Kelly doesn't think we're married. She's come back to Las Vegas."

Max could almost hear Troy snap to attention. "And yet *you* still think you got married?"

"That's the number-one question. And that's where you come in. I found out something important since I spoke to you."

This time, without Kelly's presence to stop him, Max went on to tell Troy everything that had happened to him and Kelly since the night of Troy's wedding. By the time he reached the point of finding himself in bed with her the next morning, Troy was laughing.

"So what's the problem?"

"For starters, I can't find evidence of a wedding license or a marriage certificate."

This time there was a silence at the other end of the phone. "I'll bite. What makes you think you got married then?"

"Plenty. In fact, I just saw some photographs taken the night of your wedding. They're very interesting."

Troy laughed again.

"So what's the bottom line? Are you married or aren't you?"

"What's so funny?" Max growled.

"Only that the two of you managed to exceed DeeDee's fondest dreams. That's why she cooked up a rigged garter ceremony. She'd been waiting a long time for the two of you to get together. It was a little difficult with you on the East Coast and Kelly in Las Vegas."

"Get serious," Max growled. "This means a lot to me."

"Okay. Let me get this straight. You remember marrying Kelly and spending your wedding night in the hotel's bridal suite. Right?"

"Right."

"So, outside of my congratulations on finding you married and your going to be a father, what do you want from me?"

"Come on, Troy," Max answered wearily. "I told you. Kelly doesn't believe we were actually married that night. Without some kind of paperwork to make it legal, I haven't been able to convince her. To make matters worse, her family isn't convinced either. Her policeman brother is waiting in the wings to corner me for something or another. He thinks I lied to him. Damon, another brother, will probably shoot me on sight the next time he sees me. I have to do something and do it now.''

''Good luck!''

''Thanks. The way I see it, the trail starts with you and DeeDee.''

Troy sobered. ''Yeah? I don't see how, but go ahead. How can I help?''

''The last thing I remember,'' Max went on, ''the marriage ceremony was almost over when the media people broke into the chapel and started taking pictures. After that, things got confusing. But I swear I remember a guy with a white mustache and wearing a black suit with a white collar hollering 'I now pronounce you husband and wife.'''

''Of course, that's part of the marriage ceremony. I ought to know. I was the groom.''

''Well, cousin,'' Max said wryly, ''therein lies the problem. The more I think about it, and the longer I look at the press photographs of the wedding Bennett gave me, the more I think there could be a question about that.''

''You can't be serious!''

''Think about it, cousin. Think hard!''

Troy swore under his breath. ''Oh, damn! DeeDee's going to kill me! Now that you mention it, I remember she and I ducked out of the rest of the marriage ceremony when lightbulbs started exploding. I figured I'd let you and Kelly take the heat.''

''I think you ducked too soon,'' Max answered. ''I

think the minister mistook me and Kelly for the bride and groom.''

''Yeah, maybe.'' To Max's satisfaction, his cousin sounded worried. ''I think we'd better compare notes. Where are you calling from? Boston?''

''No, Las Vegas. I'm at the Majestic, room 2511.''

''Okay. Wait for me. I'll fly out first thing in the morning and join you. We have to get to the bottom of this.''

Max hung up the phone. If the picture forming in his mind of the wedding was true, a hell of a lot of people, including Troy and DeeDee, were in for a big surprise.

He pushed the untouched room-service cart into the hallway, checked his watch and decided the best course of action was to get to bed early. If he couldn't hold the real Kelly in his arms tonight, at least he could hold her in his dreams.

MAX WAS READY and waiting impatiently when he heard Troy's voice at the door the next morning. Thank God, he murmured. Another hour of waiting and he would have been a nervous wreck. He flung open the door. ''DeeDee?''

''She wouldn't let me come without her,'' Troy muttered under his breath as he followed her into the room.

''Anything that concerns Troy concerns me,'' DeeDee announced. ''What's this about my wedding?''

''Hold up a minute, honey.'' Troy cast a pleading look at Max. ''It's Max's wedding that's in question, not ours. There's nothing wrong with ours. Right, Max?''

Max wished it was true, but too much was at stake to agree when he knew he might be wrong. From the look in DeeDee's eyes, Troy was standing on shaky ground.

''I only wanted to ask Troy a few questions about his wedding,'' Max answered. He backed away from the fire in DeeDee's eyes.

''It was my wedding, too.'' DeeDee glared at him. ''Why don't you ask me?''

Max shrugged. If a joint interview was all he was going to get, it was better than nothing. Maybe, in this instance, three heads *were* better than two. ''Come on in,'' he invited. ''Breakfast, anyone?''

''Later,'' DeeDee replied. She threw herself onto the couch. ''Where's Kelly?''

''Home.''

''Home? I don't understand. Troy told me the two of you got married the same night we did.''

''Well…'' Max eyed her warily ''Sort of.''

''What do you mean 'sort of'? Either you're married or you're not. It's like saying you're a little bit pregnant.''

''Well, that too.'' Max gave up and dropped into a chair.

DeeDee snapped to attention. ''You mean Kelly is pregnant already?''

Troy broke in. ''Wait a minute, Dee. Let's take first things first. We're here to talk about Max's wedding.''

DeeDee frowned. Max sensed she wasn't through with him—not if she thought there was a baby in the picture. The last thing he wanted to talk about was fatherhood.

"I've been replaying the night of our wedding in my mind ever since Max telephoned last night," Troy interjected. "There *was* something unusual about it."

"Like what?" DeeDee demanded. "Are you trying to say we're not married either?"

Max and Troy traded glances. "Not exactly, honey," Troy soothed. "I'll tell you about it later. Go ahead, Max. I'm listening."

Max silently handed Troy the photographs Bennett had given him.

The photographs showed Max and Kelly in the midst of a confused bridal party milling around. Photographers were snapping pictures. The minister was pointing and shouting. Troy and DeeDee were nowhere in sight.

Troy's complexion paled.

DeeDee shot out of the couch.

Troy and DeeDee stared down at the photographs. "Max?"

Max started for the telephone. "Under the circumstances, I'm going to order several pots of strong black coffee. We're going to need it."

He spread the photographs sequentially on the coffee table. "The way I read it, none of us is really married."

"That's ridiculous," DeeDee retorted. "We've just came back from a three-week honeymoon!" She grabbed the photographs, bit her bottom lip then glared at her husband. "We'd *better* be married!"

Max held up a hand when Troy started to protest. "Maybe we'd better begin at the beginning. Troy, what do you remember about your wedding ceremony?''

Troy took a deep breath, reached for one of the photographs and studied it closely. ''To tell you the truth, I didn't remember this until I saw this photograph, I swear!''

Max nodded. The photograph his cousin held was the one that had triggered his own memory. ''What didn't you remember?''

''Only that when the television-camera lights came on, I pushed you and Kelly in front of us. I was only trying to get away from the cameras, not the minister. There was so much noise and confusion I guess I didn't stay long enough to hear the minister pronounce us husband and wife.'' Troy's face was a study in misery as he examined the photograph.

Max nodded. ''So *that's* why I seemed to remember the minister hollering 'Wait a minute, I'm not through yet.' When I turned around to ask him what he was talking about, he stuck the Bible in front of my nose and shouted 'I now pronounce you husband and wife.'''

''And then what?'' Wide-eyed, DeeDee was up and staring at the photograph.

''Actually, I was in no condition to think properly or I would have straightened out the minister right away. Oh, yeah. One more thing. I vaguely remember a lot of congratulations. I must have thought it was because I caught the garter earlier and put it on Kelly. I never dreamed they were congratulating me on being married.''

He couldn't bring himself to go on to describe his reaction on finding himself in bed with Kelly the next morning. Or that they'd actively shared a wedding night. It was too personal—and too intimate to share. And so was his own "honeymoon" and the days he and Kelly had spent together as husband and wife. Days that, no matter what the outcome, he would remember for the rest of his life.

Troy sat wide-eyed while room service delivered coffee. When the door closed behind the waiter, he went on. "So you're trying to tell me DeeDee and I aren't married any more than you and Kelly are?"

Max poured himself a cup of strong black coffee to fortify himself. "It sure looks that way to me."

"Then explain it to *me*," an irate DeeDee demanded.

The answer was so convoluted, Max wasn't sure he *could* explain. He tried to gather what wits he had left. "In your case, I think your wedding ceremony was unfinished because the minister didn't pronounce you and Troy husband and wife. Did you see the minister sign your license? Did you get a signed wedding certificate?"

Troy and DeeDee traded blank glances. "No. We left before he could. Too much was going on."

"Did he mail you your wedding certificate?"

Troy shook his head. "I'm not sure. We just got back from our honeymoon yesterday. We haven't had a chance to pick up our mail."

Max threw up his hands. Another obstacle to overcome. "In my case, while the minister actually made the final pronouncement over me and Kelly, I didn't have a marriage license to begin with. So you see, it all adds up. I'd bet the farm that neither ceremony was legal."

DeeDee burst into tears.

Troy took her in his arms and tried to dry her tears. "Don't worry, sweetheart. We'll get married again. Right here, today, if you want. Right, Max?"

"Leave me out this time," Max said. He got to his feet. "The room is all yours while you decide what you want to do. As for me, I have to find a willing wife and apply for a marriage license. With luck, I won't be back tonight."

MAX PACED the entrance at the base gate while the guard checked with Kelly. After everything she'd been through in the last three weeks, he wouldn't blame her if she never wanted to see him again.

On the other hand, he hoped the photographs of their wedding Bennett had given him would show Kelly he'd been telling her what he thought was the truth all along. And prove to Patrick he wasn't a con man.

He paced the concrete walkway and cast anxious glances at the distant horizon where the O'Rourke home was hidden by trees. He'd take his cause to Kelly's father, her brothers and Father Joe, if he had to. Even Uncle Jake and Aunt Brigid. No way was he going to leave until Kelly looked him right in the eye and told him she didn't love him.

"Miss O'Rourke isn't home, sir," the guard finally announced. "Her brother Sean said she's on her way to Los Angeles. Sorry, I can't let you in."

Max cursed under his breath and headed for his car. The puzzled guard stared after him.

He hit the gas pedal with a heavy foot and headed

south to Los Angeles at eighty miles an hour—well over the speed limit.

He hadn't gone more than a mile or two when he heard a siren. A glance through the rearview mirror revealed he'd been picked up by a police car.

Damn! He pulled over and tried to put a lid on his temper. The last place he wanted to be was in a Las Vegas jail while Kelly got away.

"In a hurry?"

Max froze when Patrick O'Rourke's face appeared at the window. But he was beyond caring what the guy thought of him. If he didn't hurry, he'd miss Kelly. "Yes, I am. Give me the ticket and let me get out of here."

"I don't think so." Patrick's smile was wicked. "At the rate you're going, you could kill yourself and take someone with you. So, what's your hurry?"

"I have to catch Kelly and ask her to marry me!"

"Maybe she doesn't want to talk to you or she wouldn't be on her way to L.A."

"I swear she'll want to talk to me after I show her the photographs I have on me." Max shuffled through the pile of photographs he had on the seat beside him. "Here."

While Patrick studied the photograph, Max blurted out the truth. "Did Kelly tell you she's expecting a baby? And that I'm the father?"

Patrick studied the photograph again before he handed it back. "Follow me. We'll find her."

With sirens blaring and lights flashing, Patrick headed down the freeway with Max close behind. They caught up with her just before the California-Nevada state line. He pulled her car over.

"Patrick?" she asked incredulously when he came around to her driver's window.

"Yeah. It's me, all right. And Max. He has some photographs to show you. I suggest you talk to him." He stepped back and motioned to Max. "I'll wait back here in case you need me."

Max came around to her window and silently handed her the photographs taken at his cousin's wedding. "Here, sweetheart. These should answer a few questions."

She shuffled through the photographs. "I—I'm not sure I understand."

When Max got through explaining the wedding snafu, Kelly looked a little more cheerful. But not enough to suit him. "I was hoping those would prove I was telling you the truth when I insisted we were married. Now, all we have to do is try again."

Kelly stared at him.

"You *do* want to marry me, don't you?"

"That's not the problem, Max. You don't *have* to marry me anymore."

"*Have* to marry you?" Max was rocked by Kelly's statement. "What do you mean by that?" he asked cautiously.

"If you want to marry me for the baby's sake, you don't have to. I went to see my doctor yesterday. It seems I may not be pregnant after all. He told me it could just be stress. He said those at-home pregnancy tests could be wrong sometimes. He took a test and I'm to call him in a few days."

Max went around the car, opened the door and slid in beside Kelly. He pulled her into his arms, tenderly kissed the corners of her eyes, her lips and hugged her close. "You want this baby, don't you, Kelly?"

"More than you know." She sniffed. "So you see, if that's why you came back, you didn't have to."

"Kelly O'Rourke," Max said, smiling into her eyes. "I'm asking you to marry me as soon as possible. I'll even get down on one knee on this dusty highway and propose, if it will help you say yes. As for the baby, I have a feeling she's in there. If she's an O'Rourke, she's too tough not to be."

Kelly didn't even have to say yes. Her answering smile lit up Max's world. He ducked in through the window and kissed her with all his heart.

Unnoticed, Patrick O'Rourke's siren blared as he passed the parked car, made a U-turn and headed back to Las Vegas.

Epilogue

Kelly beamed down at her newborn daughter. "She's beautiful, isn't she?"

Max leaned over and put a forefinger in the sleeping baby's hand. When her tiny fingers curled around his, he smiled and gently kissed his daughter's red hair. "Since she's inherited her mother's good looks, yes. But she's still not quite as beautiful as you are."

Kelly blushed at his praise. "How *did* you know she'd turn out to be a girl?"

"I didn't," Max confessed with a grin. "I just felt the O'Rourkes needed another girl in their family. I just hope that when you and I have another difference of opinion, it won't turn out to be two against one."

"No more difference of opinion," Kelly vowed fervently. "Not after what it took to settle where and how we would get married. Thank goodness everyone finally agreed to the ecumenical service right here in Las Vegas. As for agreeing on the baby's name..." She gestured to the loud voices sounding outside the door. "I'm not so sure."

Max listened for a moment. "I'll be darned. My mother and your father are sure going at it." He brushed the baby's downy head and laughed when a frown wrinkled her small forehead. "She has a mind of her own, just like her mother."

"She'll love you every bit as much as I do, Max. As for our families loving her, Dad's already smitten and your mother's already bonded with her." Kelly gazed in wonder at the sleeping baby. "As for naming her, that's another story."

"Well, it seems as if we have a number of choices," Max said wryly. "Now that DeeDee and Troy have married again and are expecting a kid of their own, we can forget their input. My mother's been researching the Taylor family history for a suitable name. And then there's your father. It sounds as if he has a strong opinion about this, too. He's insisting on a good old Irish name. Take your choice, sweetheart."

"I want her to be her own person," Kelly replied. "Although, it would be nice if we named her after my mother."

"Moira?" Max considered the idea. "Sounds about right."

"And for your mother."

"Moira Andrea?" Max shrugged. "It would certainly settle the argument going on outside. And, frankly, although she won't admit it, it would tickle the hell out of my mother."

"And now that we've agreed on names for her birth certificate, what shall we *call* her? Moira Andrea is a mouthful."

"Irish," Max answered without hesitation. "After her mother."

A special feeling,
  A special secret...
    No one blossoms more beautifully
      than a woman who's

And the right man for her
will cherish the gift of love she brings.

**Join American Romance and four
wonderful authors for the event of a lifetime!**

THAT'S *OUR* BABY!
Pamela Browning
March 2000

HAVING THE BILLIONAIRE'S BABY
Ann Haven
April 2000

THAT NIGHT WE MADE BABY
Mary Anne Wilson
May 2000

MY LITTLE ONE
Linda Randall Wisdom
June 2000

Available at your favorite retail outlet.

Makes any time special ™

Visit us at www.romance.net

HARWC